Incres Islai

By

W.G.Graham

The moor had almost swallowed up the weak setting sun. Ahead of the pitiful struggling line of men and women with enough strength left after four days of pursuit by a tribe hell bent on annihilating them, Jude, their leader, halted to look back on those stragglers now too weak to go on.

Incres saw the older man wave, the gesture one of urgency, and he looked back the way they had come over a landscape of a moor pitted with bogs so wide and deep that to lose a footing would surely have ended in disaster. The Hunters were now not so very far behind, and would soon be within bow shot of the young warrior Incres and the stragglers.

"Mother, you must try once more, they are almost upon us," Incres said desperately, casting a quick glance at their pursuers and stretching out his hand to help the exhausted woman to her feet.

"No, Incres, save yourself. Help those who will see the tribe safe. I am of no use to them myself. Leave me be." The woman closed her eyes as she spoke, as if by doing so it would block out those painful last days.

Incres clutched his spear tighter, his eyes on the grey objects drawing closer. "No,"he said with a decisive shake of his head, "I will not leave you here. Not in this place."

They had been chased for the last four risings of the sun,thirty or more at the beginning, now lessened by the fingers of both hands. He heard Jude call out to him, gesturing anxiously and pointing in the direction of the nearest Hunter. Incres quickly turned his attention back to his mother.

"Come mother, you have rested enough," he said softly, bending to help her to her feet. The woman did not move. "Mother?" He put out his hand, but the woman did not respond. "Mother?" Incres knelt down, the encroaching

Hunters forgotten in his anxiety for her. He put his hand on her shoulder and, gentle as it was, the woman fell to the side.

Incres heard his leader call again, but he had eyes only for his mother, his mind racing back through the years when as a young boy she had cared for him after his father had died. How she had toiled long and hard so that he might never know hunger. How then could he leave her here in this place to be stripped of the few possession she had by the Hunters? He was not aware of Jude until the man was by his side.

"She has gone? "The leader did not wait an answer. "We must go on, there is nothing you can do for her now."

Leave her, Inces thought? That he could not do. Rain dropped harshly on the upturned face of the dead woman.

"Take what you can, Incres. The wolf skin will help keep another warm. Your mother would want that…quickly now!"

As if not wishing to disturb his mother's slumber, Incres gently took off the wolf skin cloak that he himself had brought home from his first kill, remembering her pride and joy. An arrow stuck into the dead heather a step away from where he stood.

Before Incres knew what had happened Jude gently pushed the dead woman into the bog, the brown dirty water bubbling as she sank. For a moment, as Jude stood back watching the body disappear, he thought that the young warrior would strike him. "They cannot violate her now, Incres. It will be her last resting place. The gods will watch over her."

Incres lowered his spear, his leader was right. This way they could not take from her what little she had.

"We must hurry, and if we can reach yonder hills the darkness will help hide us. "Jude started at a run, the grieving young man a stride behind him.

As they reached the rest of the column, Dryan hurried to meet them. There was no need to ask his friend from childhood what had befallen his mother. Instead he said quickly "we can reach the hills if we hurry; make a last try."

Jude brushed past the young man, urging on the nearest woman with a push to her shoulder. "Come on Woona you can do it; you're young enough," he called out harshly.

Incres half-moved to confront his leader for the way he had spoken to the girl he hoped one day to take for his own, but Dryan stopped him with a hand and a look. Now was not the time to challenge their leader.

Instead Incres came to her side. "Let me help you, Woona. "He put a hand under her arm to guide her around another pool of dirty brown water. Woona offered him a weak smile, her face twitching with the pain of every moment, and she knew she could not go on much further.

"No, Incres, help your mother." Her voice was so low that the man could scarcely hear her.

"It's all right Woona, mother is at rest with the gods now. Take this," he draped the wolf skin over her shoulder, "it will help keep you warm."

The girl halted to look into the young man's face."I...

"Keep moving, you two, it is no time for lovemaking," Jude called out angrily. "Do you want to die?"

The vision of his mother slipping so unceremoniously into that sea of mire, and the sight of Woona and those around him slowly dying on their feet, was almost too much for the young warrior.

The leader saw the hate in Incres's eyes. "Save your anger for those who deserve it," he said, pointing at the nearest Hunters leaping across the bogs, now ever closer, his voice almost soft for one who only knew the burden of leadership.

Intentionally Dryan came between them and took Woona's other arm. "Quickly now, we can all rest once we reach the hills. See, Wolf has already come to help."For the third of the three young friends was bounding back from having helped those at the front of the column. Suddenly, as he reached them, he halted, fitted an arrow to his bow and let fly at the nearest Hunter, who, with a cry clutched at his shoulder.

Although the shot had not been fatal it had the effect of halting those behind him.

"Our people have almost reached the gap between the hills. But look out!" Wolf threw himself sideways as the arrows came amongst them. Unhurt from having thrown themselves on to the ground, the men sprang up, and released their own arrows at the enemy who now numbered a score or more.

Jude hauled Woona to her feet. "Go!"he shouted at her, and as the girl stumbled through the short dead heather, swung sharply on the men." You men, make for those hills on the far side of the gap, they are not so very high. Climb as best you can. Let the Hunters see you. They will not follow if they know you are above them. Now quickly! And let Mother Darkness be our friend," he added, as more arrows flew in their direction.

Incres knew what Jude had in mind. If they were to climb beside the gap that his tribe were heading for, then he, Wolf and Dryan could prevent the hunters from following. But for how long? Should the Hunters take the chance by not halting in their pursuit but follow his tribe into the gap, then they could do little to prevent them.

Having reached the foot of the hill, the three friends, gasping for breath, started to climb. Incres almost lost his footing and had an arm reach out to haul him up. The hill was neither steep nor high, but in their weakened condition it seemed to go on for ever.

"We must reach the top!" Incres vowed.

"Have the Hunters reached the gap? Are they following close behind? Can you see, Incres?" At his side Dryan gulped in air.

Incres grasped a turf of grass and half turned to look down. He saw the Hunters split up, some to climb the hill a little further away from them and the gap, while others had halted by its mouth, knowing that Incres and his friends' arrows could reach them from that height.

"Pray for Mother Darkness, Incres."

Dryan, Incres could tell was almost totally spent. "Jude will lead the tribe to safety. The Hunters will not find them in the dark", Incres said reassuringly. He started to climb. "Come, Dryan we must reach the top."

Wolf was the first to reach the summit of their small mountain. "I think you and Dryan should see what our friends are up to who are climbing the hill to outflank us, Incres. I will remain here and see that those down there stay where they are."

"You think you can halt them on your own, do you?" Incres tried to smile at his optimistic friend.

"Who better, since you cannot hit the side of a hill with that bow of yours,"Wolf laughed as he crouched beside him.

"They will chase us through the gap. They know there are only three of us up here, and that their own fellow-Hunters will already be climbing the hill some distance beyond us."Dryan peered down into the mouth of the gap, fitting an arrow to his bow as he spoke.

His fears proved all too correct, as a handful of the Hunters took a few tentative steps into the small gap less than an arrow flight wide.

Wolf loosed off his first shot and struck someone in the midst of the emerging band; Dryan's arrow sent the remainder scurrying for the shelter of the rocks.

Wolf crawled back from the edge where he had been crouching. "I will away: - see what the Hunters are up to They won't have reached the top yet."

Incres turned his attention back to those below. "Wait, Wolf! They're making a dash to outflank us!"." The wind caught the taller man's voice, hurling it across the hilltop.

Wolf swung round, loosing off an arrow as he stood there. He saw three men go down, then a fourth. Puzzled, he threw a quick glance at Incres.

Dryan sprang to his feet and rapidly fired arrows into the melee below, adding to the confusion.

"They think it is a trap. Jude must have left some men behind,"Wolf laughed. "I think it's safe for me to leave you two here, whilst I deal with our climbing friends.

"Don't tarry too long my friend, for you may also lose us amongst these hills if Jude doesn't send someone back to guide us to them, "Incres, advised him rising to his feet

"I believe we are safe here until first light, though after that I do not know, "Jude said with a sigh.

For most of the night they had travelled through the folds of the black hills, until at last they could go no further. They had given up two children to the earth mother, and Jude feared that more of the old folk would follow should they not halt to rest. Now at last they were together again. Icy rain blown by the wind had them huddling together.

"Will it never end, Incres? "Woona asked, her voice scarcely audible above the wind, as she rested her head on the young man's shoulder.

"Some day it will end. We won't always be hunted. Some day we shall find peace - a home of our own where no one will harm us," he promised her.

Next morning Dryan ran excitedly towards them. "The Hunters have gone! They are nowhere to be seen!"

Jude heard him and left what he was doing. "You are sure, Dryan? They could be anywhere amongst these black hills."

Dryan was not to be deterred, and with a shake of his head and still smiling answered. "No, I climbed to the tallest hill I could see all around from there, even as far back as the moor we crossed yesterday."

Satisfied by the young man's assurance, Jude gave a brief nod. "We'll start now: we must find some shelter."

Although it had ceased raining during the night, Jude knew they could not go much further without food and shelter. Sadly he watched his tribe struggle to their feet; mothers clutching children to their breast, some, a little older, grasping at their mother's tattered clothing, all walking as if in a daze. Eventually they halted by a stream to drink the cold, clear water and rest for a while, Jude, ever fearful, had his warriors stand watch from higher ground. Eventually he called to them to rise and be on their way, and again he watched the pitiable band slowly rally.

"Are you all right, Woona? Shall I help you? "Incres asked anxiously as the girl stumbled and fought to regain her balance.

Woona stared at him for some time through dulled eyes, but finally gestured that she was. As she did so she saw an old woman fall, and mustering up her strength she rushed to help her, but found that she was dead.

"Take what you can. She has no need for it now. "Woona jerked around at the callous suggestion, to where Jude stood looking down at her from on the rock on which he stood.

Incres's temper boiled at the sight, yet he knew that his leader was right. The tribe had need of it more.

Later, they halted again, their rests becoming more frequent as they rapidly weakened. More of the old folk died and had to be left behind.

A grinning Wolf came running towards them, a dead rodent swinging from his outstretched hand. Jude saw him and called to a warrior to find some kindling. With guards posted they built a small fire, and watched with hungry eyes as the small animal sizzled upon the spit.

"Only the children and young women will eat," Jude ordered. "The warriors must find their own food, and should they find enough, then this they can give to the old."

Dryan caught Incres's eye. The old must starve in order to save the young, and even so there was not enough to go round from this small rodent. Jude's command had Incres wondering if he would have had the courage to make such a decision.

After the long trek across the moor and the brutality of the hills, the place which they had now found was idyllic. A lake stretched before them, pale blue in the weak sun; behind them a cliff pockmarked by caves.

Wolf trotted over to where Incres and Woona stood. "We have found a boar, and a fox, up yonder. "Wolf pointed to the cliff, his face beaming. "Tonight we will not go hungry, even the old will taste some food. I think Dryan and Marc have also found some animals sheltering in the caves."

"You believe yourself to be the great hunter, my friend Wolf?" Incres taunted, squeezing Woona's hand ,so that she too should join in the humour.

Wolf made a face. "I had more on my mind than to hold a girls hand while the true warriors of this tribe saw to it that those weaker than themselves should not go hungry, "he said in mock seriousness, staring up at the sky.

"Oh, I was not so idle that I did not have time to find these," Incres replied standing aside to display his own catch of three hares.

Wolf let out a low whistle. "I suppose it is a fair hunt," he shrugged.

"Fair?" Incres took a step towards his friend.

"Enough, you two," Woona laughed, happy that what would appear to be the worst of their travels should be over, for now they had meat and place to shelter.

"Indeed this is a good place" Jude agreed, as he stood by the edge of the lake. "Now we can fish and the forest may be useful for hunting."

"And shelter," Wolf confirmed."

"Only if the Hunters do not find us," Dryan said, dulling their spirits.

Jude turned to face the cliff. "We could defend ourselves up there, if we had to. There is one cave that would hold us all should we be attacked. We can post guards so that we are not taken unawares."

"Shall the families remain in their own caves until then?" asked Marc, the youngest of the group. Unlike Incres, Dryan and Wolf, the boy grew his hair at shoulder length which made him look older than his fourteen years.

Jude smiled, knowing what the boy meant. Despite their mutual hardships, some families did not get on together. "Yes, I think they can shelter in the caves of their choosing, until the time comes when we must all hasten to the big cave."

"We will have to store food should it come to that. "Incres spoke up for the first time. "We can salt the fish and meat we catch."

"I'll leave that to you Incres. You will be in charge of the hunters' catch."

"A wise choice Jude, "Wolf chuckled, "seeing as he is less than useless with a bow."

"As you are with a spear my friend," Incres countered.

"Enough you two. "Jude shook his head in mock dismay. "You have been at each others throats since you were at your mother's knee."

"At least I knew mine, "Wolf laughed, rapidly backing away and expecting the usual attack from his friend, though it was all done in the name of good humour.

This time Incres did not rise to the bait, instead, ignoring the good-humoured taunt, he put an arm around Marc's shoulder, and guided him away, pretending to be in deep discussion, only now and then intentionally raising his voice so that his friend would hear. "We cannot rely on Wolf, you know. It is only by luck that he has hit anything, and what he did hit must have been blind or crippled. Fortunately, there are still good hunters like you and me that the tribe can rely upon."

The boar came charging over the crest. Dryan saw it first as others stood frozen by the animal's sudden appearance, and was about to raise his spear when the mounted man came at him. Acting instinctively, Dryan swivelled round to meet this new threat, his spear taking the man in the chest and catapulting him over the rear of his mount. In a moment all were staring down at the inert figure stretched up on the ground.

"Out of my way!" Jude cried, pushing his way through the curious circle.

"He is not one of the Hunters," Incres declared, never having seen someone so richly dressed, for his clothes were not of wolf skin that he and his tribe wore, but some sort of weave."Run to the top of the crest, see if there are others!" Jude rapped out sharply to one of the men

"I thought he meant to spear me! He came from nowhere!" Dryan's eyes never left the figure on the ground.

Having heard Jude's command, Wolf had run to the crest top. "There are others some distance away!" he shouted down to the mumbling coterie.

"Quickly now, we know not who they are and it will not go well for us should they find one of their own here dead."

Nearby the dead man's horse grazed contentedly. Jude swung to Dryan. "Bring the horse here, we must put the man upon it, take him to where the lake bites into the forest; find marsh ground there and sink him. You know how to sink a man?" the leader asked a still dazed Dryan. The young man nodded nervously. "And when you have done this, remain there until someone comes for you."

Incres knew what his leader had in mind. That it would be best if Dryan was out of the way, for the shaken boy was want to give himself away.

"The rest of you: back to the caves, and be about your business as if nothing has happened, but have your weapons ready, we may have to defend ourselves," Jude urged, shooing those around him with his hands.

They had not long obeyed him before the band of riders were upon them. Jude stepped forward to meet them as if surprised by their unexpected presence.

"You are leader here? From whence have you come?" the foremost of the mounted men asked, staring belligerently down at who he clearly saw as little more than a savage.

Jude could scarcely make out the man's question so strange was his tongue. Eventually he ventured, "I am Jude, leader of the tribe Maru, and we have been driven north by those who call themselves the Hunters."

The mounted man drew himself up. "I am Meruk, lord of this land. And I too know of the Hunters."

Jude thought fast. If they were on this lord's land then undoubtedly it would mean their moving on again, to be once more at the mercy of the Hunters, or whoever was strong enough to take from them what they wanted, which was little enough. Yet he must show no weakness, for this in itself could affect this man's decision.

Jude envied him his rich clothing, and the bright sword by his side, of which he had never seen the like. Discreetly he ran his eyes over the mounted company, each similarly clothed and armed. His warriors would be no match for them, even though he knew that up in the caves arrows were at the ready. "We are in need of food and shelter. The Hunters have pursued us for many days now. We have lost a good many of our company. All that I ask is that you permit us to remain here until we are again strong enough to travel."

Meruk waved a hand as if the request was of no importance. "I search for Kan, my son. He rode after a boar in this direction. Have you seen him?"

It could not have been worse. The man Dryan had speared was this fine lord's son.

"We saw you a little way off, but believed that you had ridden in some other direction, and were startled by your sudden appearance, "Incres answered stepping to Jude's side. "But we have seen no other. Tell me: was he dressed as you are?"

Jude cleared the dryness from his throat. The boy had answered well. It would explain their false surprise at seeing these men arrive.

Meruk turned a jaundiced eye upon the boy. "Who is this that would speak to me when I address myself to your leader?"

"My father named me Incres," the young warrior answered proudly, staring this fine lord directly in the face.

Meruk curled a lip. "Then Incres, your father should have taught you that you should wait until spoken to by your betters. But no matter, you say you have not sighted my son?"

"No my lord," Jude answered quickly for he was unsure whether the hot blood that coursed through the body of this young man Incres would not come to the boil. "but should we do so, we will tell him that you are anxious for him."

Meruk pulled around his mount. "If you do, tell him that we have done this day." And with this put spur to mount.

"He did not say whether he wished us to be on our way. "Incres screwed up his eyes on the departing horsemen.

"Then we will remain here until he does." Jude let out a sigh. "Though if he were to discover that we are the cause of his son's death, we would wish that we had not."

The strange rich people did not pay them a visit as Jude and the tribe expected, neither to inquire further as regards the missing lord's son or to command them to leave their land. Jude knew the tribe was uneasy, but the bounty of the land helped to dull their fears. It had been many a long day since they had known such luxury, this, and the fact that they needed time to regain their strength.

"I should not have done it, Incres. "Dryan shook his head, his face a picture of misery as he walked by the shore that warm day. "I may only have brought destruction to our people."

"You acted in the way any of us would have done, had we been in a similar position." Incres sympathised with his friend. It would have been ill to have agreed with him in his present depressed condition. "It's of no use to brood over it, the deed is done." Incres instantly regretted his choice of words as he saw the expression on his friend's face change to one of anger.

A little distance away Woona waved and walked to meet them. "Come on, Dryan, lets have a word with Woona. I see she carries something, fruit perhaps." Dryan shrugged. He was in no mood for company, so, making his excuses he turned away.

"What's the matter with Dryan? Does he still brood over what was done?" Woona walked beside Incres as she asked the question.

Incres took her hand. "I fear he still does, Woona, and should the strange lord come again I believe Dryan will give himself…and us away, for he is so distraught."

"But it was an accident, surely. Dryan did not mean to slay the man. Don't you think it would have been best to have told that lord the truth?" Woona turned up her lip in a way that Incres loved.

"What would you have done if you were that lord, Woona, to hear that a band of strange folk had killed your son,…even in error?"

Woona nodded in understanding. "Oh, if had not happened. We are so happy here, with fish from the lake, boar and dear from the forest." She gave a deep sigh.

Incres squeezed her hand in reassurance. "As long as they do not find the body we will be safe," he said, coming to stand beside the men that Jude was addressing.

"We shall dig a ditch in front of the caves and build a ramp for us to cross. With the cliff behind us, we can defend ourselves against those who would come against us. We shall also salt what meat we have and store it in the big cave."

Jude, Incres agreed, was the wise one. It was only fitting that he should lead the tribe. Not that he had always agreed with the older man's decisions, but how would he himself have dealt with some of the more unpleasant ones that he had had to make?

The leader took his eyes from the men to watch the women at work. "We must not over-task them. They're still weak from our journeying here, and they have the children to attend to as well."

"We'll go to the forest and gather what wood we need to make arrows," Wolf said, looking at Incres for support, or his companionship.

"Do that Wolf, take Marc with you. The other men must remain here to keep watch." "Do you think they will come back?" Dryan asked, referring to Lord Meruk and his men.

"If you'd lost your son would you not return to the strangers who had mysteriously come to dwell upon your land? Should they do so, which I strongly suspect they will, I suggest, Dryan, that you make yourself scarce." Jude's words were firm, but not harsh.

"I am not afraid," Dryan answered haughtily.

"Your eyes tell me differently, and should that lord also sense this, then I fear he would instantly know of your guilt…and ours."

"It was an accident…he should…"

Jude cut Dryan short. "It is done." Then a little more gently, as if having sympathy for this unfortunate youth. "It could have happened to any of us, but since it has, then it is up to the tribe to stand against it. We are a family, and must protect our own."

It was in fact less than a week before the Lord Meruk's man came, leading a riderless horse, though the guards had spied a score or more waiting a short distance away.

"My Lord Meruk would have you accompany me to where he dwells." The man addressed Jude in a way that suggested that it was more a command than a request.

Jude acknowledged the man with a slight inclination of his head. Nearby, Wolf drew in a deep breath, for in his eyes it showed weakness.

Jude understood Wolf's look. " Have no fear, I will go with this man. "It was said in a way not only to assure his tribe of his safety, but also that he trusted this lord who had sent for him. And Incres again was aware of his leader's wisdom, for they were in no way able to resist those on the other side of the hill should Jude refuse.

To Jude, who had only once before ridden a horse, and this when a mere lad-- and that mount not so tall as this he now rode-- the ride had seemed to last forever, his discomfort immediately forgotten by the sight of what stood before him.

There on a hill stood a fortress of wood and stone, with walls, a spears length thick and twice as high, outside of which three score or more workers toiled in fields bright as the sun. Jude hid his admiration as best he could, though he had never seen such richness before.

His guide led him over a ramp and into the settlement, and Jude's eyes shone in astonishment at the conical stone houses, where smoke rose out of every roof. Twenty, thirty or more he counted from where he had dismounted. The bewildered man followed the lord's messenger to what appeared to be the largest of these dwelling, passing an enclosure of sheep, goats and cows. Clearly this man who called himself lord, had riches beyond belief.

A few whom he passed offered him a curious if somewhat sympathetic smile, whilst others drew back from this ill-clad savage.

"Wait here," his guide ordered him brusquely, and stooping, disappeared through the small entrance.

Unable to suppress his curiosity Jude took a few steps towards the nearest dwelling, where, at its door, a woman was hard at work grinding something in some sort of bowl.

"May I ask what you are doing? "he asked politely.

The woman lifted her head sharply, taking in this, to her eyes, dirty, almost indecently dressed savage. "I am grinding corn," she informed him, twisting a contemptuous lip. "You have never seen this done before?"

"Corn?" Jude raised an eyebrow.

"Corn, we grow it in the fields and bake bread with it." The voice that had spoken was that of another woman who had come up quietly behind him. She was young, smiling as she asked, "You are of the tribe by the lake, the leader of whom my father would speak with?"

Jude swallowed hard. He had no words for her beauty. She was everything that any man could desire: young, with hair as bright as the sun, skin as white as milk. "I am called Jude. "It was all he could think to say, except to wish he was many a sunrise younger.

"Then I hope you and your tribe find favour with my father. "The smile that she offered Jude was warm and genuine.

Before he could utter his thanks his guide had returned. "Lord Meruk will see you now, tribesman. "He motioned that Jude should enter.

The interior was larger than Jude had imagined. Peat smoke rose from a fire in the centre of the floor which made it difficult for him to see who else was in the room. Then, as his eyes grew accustomed to the dim light, he made out the man whom he had come to know as Lord Meruk sitting on some sort of dais, a man dressed in a long dark cloak standing by his side.

Meruk gestured to Jude to draw closer. "I give you good day, caveman." The greeting not unkindly said.

"And to you my lord, though I am no caveman, a cave dweller perhaps," Jude replied, with a hint of indignity and drawing himself to his full height.

"Perhaps not," the other conceded, "but it is of little consequence at the moment."

Jude acknowledged the statement with a slight bow, taking the opportunity to ask: "Your son has returned safe and well, I hope?" As he said it he was aware of a slight intake of breath from the man who stood next to the lord.

Meruk's eyes rested on Jude with steely suspicion. "No, he has not, though his mount returned that same day, which had me thinking, he himself must not be so very far away. I had hoped that you may have offered some news of him. A sighting perhaps? Or, that you had him safe and well, the result of him having had an accident or some such thing."

"No my lord, had this been the case I would have sent word immediately to you."

Meruk slowly nodded in acknowledgement, then asked as if having forgotten the plight of his son. "You wish to dwell by the lake?"

It was more than Jude could have hoped. "Yes, if it pleases you that we should do so."" The winter will soon be upon us, and soon the lake will be frozen over. You must catch and salt as many fish as you can, also do this with your meat. You know how to salt?" Meruk asked, raising an eyebrow.

"That we do, my lord."

"Good. Then make your preparation for the winter to come." Jude turned, sensing the interview to be at an end. "You can expect no help from us, you understand." He heard as he left.

Chapter 2

Lord Meruk had been right. The lake had frozen over with ice so thick, that a man could walk across to the opposite shore without fear of hearing it crack beneath his feet. Jude had halted the work on the uncompleted ditch, believing it to be more important to have the warriors catch whatever meat they could in order to have it salted for the encroaching winter, while the women gathered the coarse dry heather for beds and kindling.

Jude shivered: the morning was cold. The sun was covered by a grey blanket of cloud, and struggled to make itself known to the mortals shivering below. It was now the third month of snow and ice. Jude made a slow way to the lake's edge' the snow crunching beneath his feet. Here the snow was not so deep, for they had carved out a path, and each day the men would take turns to cut out a circle of ice, in the hope of taunting a fish or two to it. Today it was his turn. He shivered again. Despite their earlier hunting, they were still scarce of meat, and with the forest now naked they had no cover from which to stalk what animals remained there.

Jude's thoughts turned to the settlement he had visited those months past, especially of the girl with the flawless skin, Lyra, Meruk's daughter. The man gave a sigh, his breath hanging in the cold air. If he was only so much younger! Then he smiled to himself. Perhaps if Incres or Wolf were to find favour with her, it could end all their worries for the future. Not Incres, Jude thought again, for he had a woman in Woona, and they now shared a cave together as did most couples, though he would have preferred that they didn't in order to save wood, now that the walk through the snow to the forest seemed to take longer with each new fall of snow.

The big cave where they were all to gather in the event of an attack was open to the cold. This same cave now served to conserve the salted meat and fish stored in its bowels. Now Jude saw the foolishness of his earlier suggestion that they should all live there, as not all in the tribe lived in harmony. Besides, the younger ones like Incres and Woona preferred some privacy for their coupling.Some little distance away from the shore Jude knelt down. It would be another long day. Tomorrow he would take the warriors into the forest, and the women could gather more wood for the fires. And as Jude lifted his axe he heard the wailing of a hungry child from a cave.

At first Incres and Wolf believed them to be the carcasses of dead wolves until they drew closer; it was then that they knew that it was not so. Without so much as a word between them the young men ploughed through the powderysnow to the first lifeless black object.

Wolf was the first to reach it, turning the brown fur clad body onto its back.

"It's a man, Incres!" he cried, kneeling down and wiping snow from off the still and ashen face.

"Is he alive do you think?" Incres asked, dropping down beside his friend, as Wolf breathed into his hands before rubbing them on the frozen face.

"If he is, then it is by a sliver, "Wolf answered, his eyes still on the gaunt face and searching for any sign of life.

Incres rose. "I will see if there is life in any of the others. "The young warrior ran quickly to the next prone figure. As soon as he turned it upon its back, he knew that there was no life there. The three others that he ran to, also showed no sign of life, but the third, that of an older man, blinked up at him through the lightly falling snow.

Incres ran back to his friend. "One still lives. There is nothing I can do for him. I will fetch some of our tribesmen," he said hurriedly. Wolf watched him disappear, hoping that the snow would ease and that his friend would quickly find his way back.

It seemed forever before Incres returned with some of the other men; by that time the man whom he had first found had died, and it was the second, obviously far through, that Incres found Wolf cradling in his lap.

Dryan stooped to help one of the new arrivals lift the inert figure, and it was at that moment the near frozen man's lips moved. Dryan placed his ear close to the old man's mouth. The dying man forced out a few words, and pointed a weak bony finger. "He says there are others, in that direction." Dryan, pointed. "How far I do not know. Come on, Wolf, let's see if we can find them, but if they're in the same state as this fellow, I don't expect to find them alive."

Incres was quickly on his feet, addressing his fellow tribesmen. "Go back with our new friend here, carry him as gently as you can, and tell Jude what we are about." He turned to the others. "We will spread out, but not out of sight of one another, for it will be dark soon, and we don't know how far away these people are."

"Or if we will find them at all,."Dryan said ,stiff lipped.

"We shall, Dryan" Wolf, ever the optimist, answered. "If we don't they won't last till morning, should they be no better than our friend here."

The little band of tribesmen fanned out in an arc, and only when rounding rocks or trees were they out of sight or hearing of one another, the snow falling ever thicker as they journeyed on.

"Should this snow keep up, we may not see them at all, for they could be buried beneath it and us passing within a spear's length of them, "one of the tribe suggested, lifting a foot knee high to stamp it down again in front of him.

"It will soon be dark as well. "Dryan blew warmth into his cupped hands.

"We'll see by the moon's light, Dryan." Wolf confirmed his optimism with a smile.

Dryan gave him a stare to match the coldness of the evening. How he disliked him at times like this! Why could he not for once recognise the seriousness of the situation?

They were about to give up and turn for home before the last of the daylight had faded, when Arno called from the furthest flank of their arc that he had found something or someone. Struggling through the snow they converged on a half covered body, and once again went about finding out whether their discovery was alive or not. This one was not. It was as they stood there that Arno noticed the glimmer of light through the driving snow. "There, Incres, there!" the big man shouted at them, already starting towards it, Incres and the others following. The light that they had seen came from the shelter of a small copse, where a dozen or so people huddled around a small fire. Dryan was the first to reach them, none bothering or caring to acknowledge his presence.

Clearly shaken, Dryan halted. "Are they dead, Incres?" he asked staring, for none had risen to greet them.

"No, Dryan the fire did not light by itself, they are past caring whether they live or die," Incres said softly, moving closer.

Slowly, as if fearing that all here were spirits of dead ancestors, the tribe moved in amongst them. At last one lifted his head and stared at these strangers with uncomprehending eyes. "We have come to help," was all Incres could think to say.

The staring man did not move. Slowly at first another turned his face towards them, raising a weak hand in acknowledgement. "You may have not come in time my friend. We can go no further."

At last Incres was aware of others arousing themselves as if here at last was perhaps some glimmer of hope that they could be saved. "Build the fire higher, have some men help you, Arno," Incres commanded sharply.

"How will we get them back home Incres? There are too many for us to carry," Wolf had asked, coming to stand by his friend.

"We must do what we can. Someone must fetch Jude; he will decide what best to do."

Mercifully the snow had eased and now that the fire was higher, Incres and some of his band started to help those whom he thought could make the journey back to the caves. Incres looked at those who were left, and as he did so an old man gently slid sideways into the snow, and Incres thought that there would be others who would soon follow, especially if Jude; providing that he could find their tracks, did not soon come to their rescue.

Jude soon came, and with him all of the remaining warriors and three women, who had volunteered to help. It was not until close to a new day that they eventually brought all who had survived in sight of the caves.

"You must share your dwellings with our new friends," Jude told his tribe abruptly, for now almost totally exhausted himself he was in no mood for dissension.

Wolf winked at Incres. "No coupling tonight,my friend, I fear."

Incres gave a scowl. "You should know about that, my friend" for Wolf shared with Dryan and Arno.

Woona ran to meet them. "How many more are there, Incres?" she asked anxiously, her eyes on those stumbling towards the caves.

"I'm not sure, Woona; we have lost some on the way."

"I should have come to help, but Jude asked me to stay behind to help light the fires and have meat on the spits for their coming."

Having heard what the girl had said, Jude shuffled towards them. "I would have them settle in the big cave, but not tonight. It is to the smaller dwellings that they must go, and if they're crowded, so much the warmer."

While the leader spoke, Woona's eyes drifted to where a frail young boy and girl stood shivering in the pale light of the moon. "We must look after those children, Incres." She did not halt to hear his reply, but instead hurried to them, taking them by the hand and bringing them back to where Jude and Incres still stood.

Inside their small cave Woona rapidly went about stripping the young girl of her wet clothes and replacing them with dry ones of her own, while Incres did the same with the boy. Now the children sat with their eyes half closed with exhaustion and the heat of the fire. Incres rubbed some life into the boy's hands, who in turn gave a moan as the circulation returned, while Woona turned the meat on the spit.

"I think they are both too tired to eat, Woona." Incres's eyes were on the children whom he thought would have devoured the meat they had handed them, but instead chewed slowly as if even this too, was too much of an effort.

"They will be hungrier in the morning, let them sleep, "Woona said, gently taking the piece of meat out of the hand of the dozing girl.

"I wonder what has happened to their mother and father? "Incres covered the boy with a wolf skin, tucking it under his chin, as he spoke.

"This we shall find out in the morning, Incres. Now let us have some sleep as well."

The snow had halted during the night, leaving the morning cold and crisp, a weak sun struggling to make itself known to the land.

Jude found the leader of those they had rescued. He was a short well built man who struggled to rise when Jude entered the small cave. Jude gestured that he should remain where he was. "My name is Jude, I am leader here. You have slept well?"

The other drew his wolf skin tightly around him and gave a little shiver. "Yes, and I thank you, and yours for saving our lives. My name is Tomolon, and I too am leader of my tribe, the Braskan." He made a face. "Or what is left of it." Again he started to rise. "I must find out how many of us have survived, though if it was not for your tribe, there in fact would be none." "I'm only too happy that our hunters found you. But tell me, Tomolon, where have you come from, and to where do you journey?"

The man rose stiffly, gasping for breath "Where we were going , that is something none of us knew, for our only aim was to keep as great a distance between us and those who call themselves 'The Hunters.' You know of them?" he asked at Jude's sharp intake of breath

"It is why we ourselves are here," Jude answered sourly. "Though it must be said it has been for the better, at least for the present, for we live here at the sufferance of a rich leader by the name of Meruk."

"Rich you say?"

Jude nodded, and told him briefly of the settlement with its great stone dwellings-of cattle and something they called corn from which they baked bread.

"This is something I must see for myself."

Outside, Incres gave a laugh at the boy standing there, the skin that he had given him almost reaching to his ankles. The boy's sister did not join in the fun.

Woona put her arm around her as they stood outside of the cave. "Where is your mother and father, Gista?" she asked, having learned the girl's name that morning.

"They died when we were chased by the Hunters," she replied dolefully, drawing closer, as if having found a new mother in this girl who had shown her kindness.

"Then you and your brother Yan shall stay with us," Woona said determinedly, looking at Incres, and challenging him to defy her, a mere woman.

"We must wait and see what their leader has to say about this," he said.

"Surely he will not expect to leave in this weather, Incres, not while they are so weak?" Woona's eyes widened in astonishment at the thought. "Besides, where will they go?"

"That is for him to decide," Incres replied crisply, for this was not woman's business

As the camp stirred to go about its daily tasks, Jude, threw back the deerskin that covered the cave entrance wherein sat the hunched Brascan leader . "I will take you to the big cave when you have seen to your tribe. I think it best that you take them there until it is time for you to leave. Yet I do not think it will be for some time, as your people are still weak, and the weather shows little sign of easing."

"I thank you, Jude." In truth, the man himself had little strength left in him, but as leader he knew that he had to see how many of his tribe had survived.

One of his warriors came trudging through the snow to Tomolon as he stepped out of his shelter. "Three have died during the night, Tomolon. "He greeted his leader with a slight bow, reeling off the names of those who had not survived the ordeal.

"Have you counted how many of us are left?" Tomolon asked of the man, hoping the news would not be as bad as he expected.

"Nine warriors, eight women and now that I have seen Yan and Gista, four children. Only two of the old folk have survived. We should take away our dead, put them in the big cave there until the ground is soft again," he suggested, looking at Jude, who returned the look with a shake of his head.

"That is where we store our meat. Also, it is where I have told Tomolon that you may stay until you are well enough to journey on. We will help you to take your dead up yonder." Jude pointed to a small hill some little distance away. "We will bury them deep in the snow, so that no wolf will disturb their slumber."

"I thank you Jude," Tomolon answered for his warrior.

"Go back to the caves where you slept last night, and you can do so again tonight." Jude told him.

"Tomorrow, we will go to the forest and bring back timber for your fires, then, when you are better rested you can hunt with my warriors. "

As the tribesemen went about their business, Dryan said to the others in a far from optimistic tone: "We have scarcely enough food to fill our own bellies. How are we to fend for these new strangers who cannot hunt for themselves?"

"They will when they have rested, "said Incres reassuringly.

Wolf put a hand up to shield his eyes from the weak sun. "It will not be long now until the snow melts."

"How do you know this, oh definer of signs?" Incres mocked his friend in a humorous tone. "I have read the signs, "Wolf replied in pretended seriousness as he trudged through the snow towards the forest by the lake side.

"You mean, the birds flying to the north again? "Dryan asked shading his own eyes.

"No, because Arno has just fallen through a crack in the ice!" Wolf laughed, as they all turned to see the unfortunate man clambering ashore from where he had been fishing through a hole close to the shore. Arno saw them laughing at him and made a gesture which had them laughing again.

"It is just as well that he was not so very far from the lake's edge, "Dryan commented in his usual despondent manner. "Should we warn the others?"

"I think they already know. "Wolf laughed at the sight of his fellow tribes-people stopping work to see the fun.

"It is good to laugh," Dryan sighed.

"Then when are you going to start, Dryan?" Incres put a friendly hand on the lad's shoulder, and laughing pushed him away.

It was next day when all changed for the ever-despondent Dryan. Holding the leather satchel under the broken ice, the girl scooped water into it. She did not see the man until she had turned from her task.

"Can I carry that for you?" Dryan asked. Then he saw her face, to him the most beautiful he had ever seen. Now there was no need to be jealous of Incres with his Woona. As she stood there the warmth of her smile had Dryan's heart throbbing.

"It's not heavy, but you can if you wish."

Dryan's hand shook as he took the proffered water skin. "You won't have yet fully recovered from your ordeal," he choked. Stammering awkwardly, he went on: "My name is Dryan."

She gave a little nod. "Mine is Myna."

"It is a good name. "It was all he could think to say. "You are alone? Or have you hinfolk?"

"My father and mother died from a sickness many years ago when I was little. My grandfather was killed by the Hunters before you found us." They had almost reached the slope to the caves before the girl spoke again. "It is so peaceful here, ….safe too. I hope Tomolon does not have us leave too soon."

It was also what Dryan was thinking. Until he had met this lovely creature he was anxious that these folk should leave. He had privately felt that they had scarcely enough to eat for themselves without having to feed extra mouths, but now it suddenly seemed different; they could hunt longer, bring in more. In truth it was only this girl he was thinking of, the rest of her tribe could leave, and gladly, if she were to stay. And why not? She had no kin, or so she said. "It would not be wise to go on until you have all regained your strength and the weather lightens, Myna." He said her name again under his breath. Suddenly the gods had been kind to him.

Next day as the three friends made their way home from the forest, Wolf gave a far from silent chuckle.

"What amuses you, friend of mine?" Incres asked with a suspicious smile, hitching his day's hunting higher on his shoulder.

Wolf gave Incres a wink for Dryan's benefit. "Dryan is in love. Her name is Myna." "How do you know what she's called?" Incres asked, stepping around a tree stump.

Wold smiled mischievously. "It's the name that has been on his lips all day, and nothing else, not even a morsel of food. He has been struck by the gods."

"When you are struck it will not be by the gods, my aggravating friend." Dryan pushed his shoulder against Wolf, almost dropping the deer he was carrying.

Jude was unhappy, each day there was less food, and game was harder to find now that they had to hunt further into the forest. Soon it would take most of the short day to reach their new hunting ground. It had been easier at first, following their tracks in the snow, but now that most of the snow had melted, game was harder to find, everything seemingly having gone to ground.

The new tribesmen were now in the big cave. Together they had built a wall of timber and stone at the entrance to keep out the bitter winds, but the place was too big to keep in any sort of heat. Jude had gone there after the days hunting to find them huddled around the fire. Although it had grieved him to see such a pathetic sight, and hear the wailing of the children, he knew that anger would soon flare up from his own tribesmen, should he ask them to share their homes any longer. It had not been a few who eyed these people who had come amongst them with a suspicion that they might be tempted to help themselves to the meat stored there. If this happened, he feared there might be bloodshed, and he would be forced to ask the Braskan to leave.

"We will ask Tomolon to take his people away when the weather is kinder," Jude said softly to the three friends when they came back from a particularly pitiful days hunting, for he did not want the strangers who had helped in the hunt overhearing what he had to say.

"But where will they go?" Dryan was aghast at the thought that he might lose Myna.

"That is for them to decide," Jude answered abruptly, although secretly ashamed that he might be sending them to their death, especially the very young and old amongst them.

Dryan was lost in his own thoughts. Perhaps Myna would not leave with her tribe. And why should she? Though he knew he had little to share with her, nothing to give, except his love of course. Even so, it had been the same at first with his own parents, his father had told him when his mother had died. And had they not been happy?

Unexpectedly Meruk rode in to Jude's camp; this time he had two score mounted warriors at his back. Apprehensively Jude walked to meet him. The snow had cleared and the earth was coming to life again. Meruk jerked an angry finger at the strangers. "Who are these people who would settle upon my land without permission?"

Aware of the absence of any greeting from the man, Jude balked at the question. Yet he must not show fear. "We sheltered them when they were being chased by the Hunters, my Lord Meruk. They call themselves the Brascan. There was no insult intended: I would have informed you as soon as the weather cleared."

Meruk took a deliberately long look at the sky. "The weather has cleared, and no one of your tribe has come to tell their lord of this thing of which you speak."

"It was in my mind to do so. Today, because it is fine, we had need to hunt. We have little left to eat, especially since we are greater in numbers, for there are many young and old who cannot hunt for themselves."

"Then those should be cast out to provide for the strong. It is the only way," Meruk replied haughtily.

Appalled by this callous thought, Jude stared at this rich mounted man. "It is not the way of the Maru. We are not savages, my lord."

To his surprise Meruk smiled down at him. "Despite your dress you are not." He gave a chuckle. "These strangers, they mean to stay here?"

"This is something that only their leader can tell you, my lord," Jude answered, gesturing to Tomolon to come forward.

"And you are?" Meruk's eyes ran over the nervous man.

"Tomolon, my lord."

"And tell me Tomolon of the Brascan, do you wish to remain here under my protection? Or do you intend to resume your journey?"

"With your permission we would like to make this our home. Should that sit well with Jude and his people," he asked hopefully.

At this Dryan gave a sharp intake of breath. It was the first he had heard of this, that they intended to stay. Now he would have Myna to himself. So he must find some suitable place for them to live.

"Is it not your custom to offer a refreshment to your lord?" Meruk's brown eyes drifted from the leader of the Brascan to Jude, then laughing at his own humour dismounted.

"No good will come of it my lord." Meruk glared at his first warrior. The man was always the pessimist. Now he will tell him how he had had a dream, and the gods saw nothing but evil in these men who were drilling in the meadow outside of the settlement. "Once there were but nine warriors, now they number a score or more," Emgot went on, his agitation having him wave his cup of wine, so that some spilled on the earthern floor of the house. He saw that his lord was annoyed and hastened to soften his words. "You are over generous. First, you let them settle on your land, then, when there are more of them you let them also settle. Then, as if your kindness has no bounds you help clothe, and show them how to build houses of stone like these." Emgot the warrior pointed his cup at the roof. "And plant corn."

"You see ill in this, Emgot? They are not savages. This much I found out when I put the question to Jude their leader, that he cast out those of his tribe not strong enough to earn their bread. The look he gave me was not one that I am likely to forget. It was a look that said that it was I, Meruk, who was the savage."

"But my lord, should they turn against you what then?"

"Turn against me?" Meruk was puzzled. "Why should they sever the hand that protects them?"

"Perhaps if they thought you weak enough, they might take an arm." Meruk chuckled at Emgot's metaphor.

"Let me explain my reasons to you, Emgot. Jude and his tribe are a half days ride away. Should the Hunters, or any such foe decide to attempt to take our land, these so called savages of yours will be the first to know, and hence to warn us. And a score more warriors will always help."

"That is if they do not turn tail and run to save their owns skins," Emgot added sourly. "And if they do, which I think it most unlikely, then where better than here, to our home, would you not say?"

With this, Emgot the first warrior believed that once again his warnings had gone unheeded by this over kindly lord of his.

Stripped to the waist in this warm Spring day, the three friends waited as Meruk's warriors of the Asan came down the line, dropping a long sword and a round shield at each of their feet. "Pick them up!" the sword master ordered sharply. Now, he thought for some fun, for by the look on the faces of these savages they had never seen weapons such as these before.   Standing next to Incres, Dryan was uneasy. Jude had carefully mulled over whether to let him come or not, but then decided the man had no choice, for it would have been suspicious had he not done so. Besides, it was a command by their overlord.

After the sword master had had his fun as predicted, the three sat by the small river that ran at the foot of the bank from the settlement.

"Give me the bow every time," Wolf said wearily, inspecting the blisters on the palm of his hand.

"That counts for me as well," Dryan agreed, lying back on the short grass.

Incres stared down at the river where some of the women were drawing water. "I think it is an art that one day we will be happy to have learned. The swords are of a metal of which I have never seen.

Even the Hunters have nothing that compares, though their weapons are better than our own. Have you noticed that we are not allowed to venture near where they are made? This must be a great secret of theirs. "He would have continued had his eyes not rested on a young woman carrying a jar of water. She was the most beautiful he had ever set eyes upon.

"We will sleep well tonight again, especially after the feast they give us every night," Dryan was saying. "They mean to make us well and strong. But why, so that we may die when our Lord Meruk decides to raid another tribe?"

"That is not the manner of the man," Incres said slowly, his eyes following the lovely girl as she drew closer.

"Where are you off to?" Wolf asked lazily as Incres rose. "We will be back to practice in a short time." His last words followed his friend as he strode purposely to the approaching girl. Lyra ignored Incres, and made to pass him as he halted before her. "Allow me to carry your pitcher, it would appear to be heavy for one so young and delicate, not to say, beautiful."

The young warrior had never expressed himself with so many flowery words before, but never had he been so enchanted.

"It is no heavier than it was yesterday or the day before," came the cold reply. Who was this savage to speak to her in such a manner? The flesh would be stripped from his back should her father find out. Yet, as she looked at his bare torso, there was something about this man. Perhaps he was not a savage as were others of his tribe?

"No, that was stupid of me," Incres conceded. "I ask your forgiveness."

"That you will have, if you will just let me pass."

Incres stood aside. "Shall I see you here tomorrow? Do you fetch water at this time every day? "he asked anxiously, hurrying to match her stride, and aware that his two friends were watching him with amusement.

"It will be the same again tomorrow," Dryan sighed, as he and his fellow tribesmen lay on the course dead heather beds in one of the larger of the black dwellings used to house them. He missed Myna, and longed to be back home beside the lake and his own tribe. This, and the fact that he was apprehensive of giving himself away. He gave a little shudder, and bit his lip at the thought of Meruk discovering that it was he who had killed his son.

"Do you intend being a builder of stone houses?" Wolf asked, as if the question was of the greatest importance to him, though he had to ask the question again before Incres realised that it was he to whom he spoke.

"Eh?"

"You mean to build dwellings such as this?" Wolf asked again, jerking his head towards the roof."

"What manner of question is that to ask, you idiot?" Incres asked, annoyed at the interruption to his thoughts, unaware of having sat staring at the roof for some time. Now understanding Wolf's attempt at humour, Incres drew up his knees to his chin and drew in a deep breath. "She is the most beautiful creature the gods have ever put upon mother earth."

"The man is love-struck, for I know who he means," Wolf mocked, shaking his head and smiling at the others there. "Does not one of us here also have eyes for her? She is not for any of us savages, Incres; not when she is the Lord Meruk's daughter."

Incres turned his head to stare at his friend. "But she drew water as if she was one of them...not..."

"A princess?" Wolf suggested with a grin.

Dryan placed a hand upon Incres's knee. "Have a care my friend, not only would it be dangerous for yourself, but for all of us should Meruk come to know of this....especially...." Incres understood what Dryan meant. It would only take an unguarded word to let the Asan know of Meruk's son's death and all would be different.

"Does one woman not content you, Incres?" Wolf was serious for once.

It was then that Incres realised for the first time that he had not thought of Woona all that long day.

"Why do you not take me with you to the settlement?" Woona

asked sullenly, for Incres had journeyed there many times since his training had ended, and each time that she had asked, he had answered her with some sort of excuse or other. Today, the excuse was that the journey was too long. This, and the fact she would slow him down, and he would have to spend the night there, when all he wanted was to be with her. Other times it had been that she had enough to do caring for Gista and Yan, whom she now looked upon as a younger brother and sister. Incres was worried that Woona would eventually suspect that he had other reasons for not taking her when he and some others of the tribe carried the meat and salted fish, which they traded for cloth and earthen ware, but he just had to keep on seeing Lyra.

That he was playing a dangerous game did little to deter him. At first Lyra would have nothing to do with him, always appearing to look at him with disdain, but somehow; he could not remember exactly how it had happened, she had deigned to speak to him. Thereafter, he had made it his business to secretly seek her out whenever he called at the settlement.

"We must be more cautious Incres." Lyra scrubbed the cloth on the rock with all the vigour she could muster. She was afraid, not for herself but for this man she had come to care for, looking for him whenever the gate opened and his tribesmen entered with their wares.

Incres examined his pony's hoof as if this was all that concerned him. "Will we ever be alone, Lyra?" he asked, letting the hoof drop and looking around him to see that no eyes were upon them.

The girl halted in her work. "You wish more?"

"Of course." Incres brought his look back to her.

"And if I do not? I am daughter to the Lord Meluk and could choose any man that my heart desires."

"And does it not desire me, as I you? "Incres was growing angry now, or was it just impatience. "So ,if you can have any man as you say, why linger here with me?"

Lyra cocked her head to one side. "Perhaps you have what other men lack" she said teasingly.

"That you will never know my precious, since we will never be alone."

Incres had no option but to do as Jude had told him, that Woona must travel to the settlement with the rest of the women, for today almost all the tribe were needed to carry their first crop there, whilst he himself remained behind. It would do Incres good to understand the meaning of responsibility he thought.

Myna gave Dryan an almost apologetic smile when she told him that she was going to the settlement and that he had been left behind to guard the camp, not realising the real meaning behind Jude's decision.

"Give her a hug and let's be on our way," Wolf taunted his friend as he passed.

"We will not be back tonight, Dryan. Can you live without me that long?" Myna gave a pert little smile, eyes twinkling as she awaited her man's answer.

Understanding her game Dryan shrugged. "I will probably be so busy I will not miss you. Besides, I have Gista and Yan to attend to now that Woona is going with you. That should keep me busy."

"Oh you…" Myna gave him a playful push.

"Come on Myna, the others are already leaving!" Woona called out to her.

Lyra heard the murmur of those closer to the gate as she walked beside her father.

"It is the tribesmen from the lake," Meruk said, halting to watch the first of those entering.

"Their tribe has no name, father?" She had never thought of it before and had never thought to ask Incres.

"They name themselves the Maru," Meruk answered off-handedly.

Lyra saw Incres lead the laden pony through the gate, but it was the girl by his side that her eyes settled on. This must be the one whom he shared with. The one he had said he had known since childhood. Did he love her? she had asked, and to her surprise she had found her heart beating rapidly as she awaited his answer.

The question seemed to have puzzled Incres, she remembered, for he had furrowed his brow as he answered that he had never given it much thought.

Lyra studied the girl walking and laughing beside the one she was beginning to fall in love with. She was not as pretty as herself, in fact she was ugly. How could Incres possibly couple with such as that? When she had asked that same question of him, he had shrugged, saying that warriors must choose someone, as it was the way of preserving the tribe. Some, he had said, had two partners but only to couple with. She had been aghast at this. How could any woman share her man with another? Perhaps they were savages after all? She gave a little shiver.

To Lyra's dismay, Incres strode towards her. She held her breath. He had come alone, leaving the others by the gate, their ponies stamping impatiently. Women of his tribe who had never been here before stood staring and pointing in wonder at the various strange things around them.

"Greetings, Lord Meruk." Incres halted, giving a deep bow. "I bring you our first harvest. I hope it pleases you."

Meruk acknowledged Incres's greeting with a nod. "It would appear to be an abundance of corn, much more than I expected from your first crop."

"Thanks to you my lord who taught us how it should be done."

Meruk accepted the flattery with a smile. "Come Incres, let us take wine, we have much to discuss you and I." As he turned to lead Incres away, Lyra threw him a brief smile of welcome.

With Woona beside him most of the time, Incres could not find a way of meeting Lyra. It was not until the evening that the opportunity presented itself. Under the pretence of having been summoned by the lord himself, he had made to leave the shelter when, stooping through the low doorway, Wolf had caught him by the arm. "I know that the way of our tribe is for a woman to accept more than one man into their beds, this has always been a way to ensure our survival," he whispered. "Yet I do not believe Woona will do so, not in this way. Have you thought what will happen should Meruk find out that you secretly meet with his one and only daughter, you a savage? And should you have the good fortune to survive his wrath, I do not think you will carry that same good fortune with you when Woona hears of this."

Incres knew what Wolf said was the truth, but the fire in his belly every time he thought of Lyra far out- weighed the wrath of both Lord Meruk or Woona. Shrugging off Wolf's grip, and unable to answer his friend, Incres ducked through the doorway.

The clouds hid the moon as Lyra waited for him by the river. She waited eagerly as he ran to her. Somehow the risk of being discovered with this savage seemed of little consequence to her. Yet, what would be Incres's fate, if her father were to find out, for she knew her father's wrath as well as his kindness. Lyra was in his arms smothering him with kisses. He drew back to smile down into her upturned face, and his heart beat ever faster, as she spoke.

"I did not think that you would come, not when you had that woman by your side. But what are we to do, Incres; we cannot keep our love a secret forever?" Lyra snuggled her face into his chest.

Love...love, Incres could scarcely believe what this beautiful creature had said. He drew back his head a little to gaze down into that lovely face. "You truly love me, Lyra?" he choked "If this is so, then we must tell your father."

Lyra let out a startled cry as she freed herself from the man's embrace, and stared at him as if he had lost his senses. "That you cannot do, Incres, he would have you slain, if not tortured first, for even having the".....she knew the word she should use was bravery, but this is not what her father would see it as.

"You think that I am too much of a coward?" Incres drew her closer.

She shook her head. "No, never that Incres, but my father has more in mind for me than...." She knew by his hurt look that her choice of words had been a mistake and hastened to amend them. "Emgot would have me wed Shaman, Lord of the Gantu in order to form an alliance. My father will not hear of it, for he hates that tribe, almost as much as he loves me."

Incres stared at his feet, the pleasure of being with her now all gone. "And you? Do you know this man….. like him?" he asked, afraid to have said the word love, his voice no more than a whisper.

"I have scarcely met the man, but, should my father change his mind so that both our tribes may live in peace, it may well be my duty as his daughter to do so." She was close to tears as she touched Incres on the shoulder, imploring him to look at her.

"Then knowing this, why did you agree to meet me, have me believe that you had some affection for me…a savage?" He jerked his head up to stare at her angrily.

"I do Incres, don't ask me how it happened but it has. Though there is no future for us, except what we have this night." Lyra drew him down to her as she slid to the ground.

Next morning Wolf ignored his friend, for he was angry that Incres had returned late and that he had been with Lyra, as he was in no doubt, by the grin Incres had given him as to what had transpired between him and the girl.

It was not that he was just angry with his friend, but particularly what he was doing to Woona, a girl who had cared for him since, and before Incres' mother had died. Now he had betrayed her by sneaking off into the night to be with someone else.

They heard a commotion from outside, and Wolf rose. "There seems to be some sort of trouble outside," he called out. Yawning, the men of the tribe roused themselves. The women, they believed, were no doubt already at work preparing their breakfast.

The chill of the morning hit Wolf as he stepped outside. Across the open square, guards were dragging a woman in the direction of Meruk's house. At first he believed it to be some sort of domestic quarrel, until he heard someone scream the name Incres, and he was running in that direction, for now it could be none other than one of their own, and that someone he was certain was Myna.

Without thinking, Wolf launched himself at the nearest guard who held the girl, throwing the unsuspecting man back, and before the second guard had time to know what was happening he had pulled Myna to his side. "What are you about? What is the meaning of this? "Wolf hurled angrily at the guards as others hurried to see what the fuss was all about. Now others of his tribe were hurrying to his aid, Incres amongst them.

The guard whom Wolf had attacked was now on his feet, sword drawn. Unarmed, Wolf could only glare at him. Then, despite his earlier anger at his friend, he felt a flood of relief as Incres came to stand by his side.

"You will answer to Lord Meruk for this,…savage," the guard threw at him. Now other Asans were running across the square.

Incres swept an anxious look round him. "We have no weapons and are outnumbered, Wolf, should it come to a fight. But why?"

Before the sobbing woman could answer them, Lord Meruk's first warrior, followed by a dozen or so others came striding towards them.

"What it is?" Emgot snapped, glaring at those nearest him, then to the guard with drawn sword. "You!" The word a command.

The guard coloured, and lowered his weapon. "It's a matter that I believe should be for the ear of my lord alone."

Clearly insulted by the remark Emgot raged at the man. "Tell me and at once. Am I not My Lord Meruk's first warrior?"

Although the guard was clearly afraid of his superior, he held his ground. "I mean no disrespect … but I do not believe my lord would wish that I tell you here…" he gestured at the ring of spectators.

The confrontation was halted by the presence of that lord himself, the coterie of curious spectators rapidly giving way as he strode to their midst.

"My Lord Meruk." Emgot gave a slight bow. "This man here will not obey my command, by telling me why he had taken this woman." He pointed to where Myna had hidden herself behind Wolf.

Crooking his finger, Meruk ordered the warrior to step forward.

"My Lord." The man kneeled. "I did not wish to disobey Emgot, but I thought it best that what you are about to know was for your ear only."

Incres felt his heart fluttering. Was his and Lyra's love a secret no more? His eyes searched for her, and when he could not see her, feared the worst. But why Myna? Was it her who had betrayed them? It was then he felt the presence of Woona beside him, her arm around a sobbing terrified Myna.

"Tell me at once, man," Incres heard Meruk demand of his guard.

His head still bowed, the man rose. "Very well my lord." His words were scarcely audible above the excited muttering of the crowd. He turned and gestured that Myna should step forward. Incres heard her stifle a cry and he took her gently by the arm and led her forward.

As they did so, the guard snatched at her hand, almost overbalancing her as he pulled her towards his master, at the same time as Wolf held Incres back who was about to come to the girl's aid.

Now in front of Meruk, the girl sobbed uncontrollably, her eyes firmly fixed on the ground as the guard lifted her hand and held it so that his master could see.

Incres saw Meruk's face twitch, in turn to be contorted with rage, so that even he felt afraid. "Where did you get that?" Meruk barked, stepping forward to yank the ring off the sobbing girl's finger. Terrified, Myna still did not answer. "I'll ask you again, girl. Where did you get this ring of my son? "Meruk held up the ring to her.

Wolf heard Woona gasp, and he saw Incres's back straighten as he stood there beside the accused girl. Myna shook her head, clearly not understanding what this was all about.

"Do you wish me to have you tortured, girl?" Meruk barked, glaring at her. For a moment Incres feared that he would strike the terrified girl.

"Dryan gave it to me." So low were the words that even Meruk who was closest to her had to ask her to speak up. Again the name Dryan tumbled from her trembling lips.

"It is as I have said, my Lord; it is the savages who you have treated as you would your own who have murdered your son! "Emgot cried out, so that all might hear, a gleam of triumph on his face at the angry growl of the crowd.

Meruk spun round to confront Incres and those of his tribe. "You all knew of this?" he asked, his eyes on Incres as if acknowledging him as spokesman.

"This we did my Lord, but the slaying of your son was an accident. He came at us over the hilltop spear couched. Dryan being nearest believed himself to be at risk and defended himself. It was only later that we realised that he was in chase of the boar."

Meruk cut him short. "And my son…what did you do with the body of my son?"

It was time Wolf thought that he too must share the burden of this inquisition. "We buried him by the lake My Lord," he said firmly, stepping to Incres's side.

Meruk seemed to sag a little, gesturing as he swung away. "Have them all held under guard…the women as well."

They held them in the same dwelling in which they had spent the night, none knowing what their fate might be, and it was not until the sun was dipping behind the distant hills, that they were again brought to the square, little having been said as they sat in the house awaiting their fate. Even the ever optimistic Wolf had remained silent.

Wolf at last gave Incres a weak smile and a wink as the women sobbed and hugged one another. It would not be long now before they knew what was before them.

Across the square from where Incres and his tribe waited, the gate creaked open and a horsemen appeared, dragging a figure behind it. The figure rose, and as the horse spurred forward was dragged to his knees to fall again on to his belly.

"Dryan" Wolf murmured. "Meruk has had him brought to him."

Incres watched as other mounted guards entered, amongst whom they recognised as Jude and Tomolon.

Again Dryan struggled to his feet, his glazed eyes unfocused, as if already having accepted his fate. This time however, his bonds were struck off and he was hauled by his shoulders by two guards to be pushed to the ground in front of the Asan leader.

"It was you who slew Kan my son?" Meruk asked the kneeling figure in a soft voice. Dryan raised his head defiantly. "This I did, but only to save myself. It was an accident My Lord, of this I swear."

"He lies to save his worthless skin," Emgot roared at the kneeling man.

Meruk gestured impatiently at his first warrior. Again he addressed his captive. "This I can accept, though you left me to grieve as to the fate of my son, and where his final resting place may be."

Here Meruk lifted his eyes to sweep to those awaiting their fate, before travelling to Jude and Tomolon. However, what I cannot accept is that you would also rob him!" Meruk's voice rose as it filled with anger.

"Kill them all, my Lord!" Emgot screamed. "They were all party to your son's murder.

The warrior's accusation brought an angry murmur of agreement from his own tribe, and some stepped eagerly forward to do his bidding.

"Jude means to do nothing," Incres whispered to Wolf by his side. "He will let them kill Dryan."

"What can he do? What can any of us do?" As he spoke Wolf grasped Incres's arm as he made to start forward. "Do not lose your own life as well, my friend Incres."

"What Wolf has said is right, Incres, we can do nothing except to lose our own lives." Woona slid her hand into his.

"It is all of my doing," Myna sobbed. "I should have told him nothing."

"What is done is done," Wolf sighed. "It is as much Dryan's doing as your own."

While they spoke Dryan had been dragged and tied to a large wooden stake.

"No!" Myna screamed, rushing forward, all her fear gone in an attempt to save her lover, until caught and held by the guards.

Incresdid not see Meruk give the signal, but heard only the screech from Myna and a howl of pain from Dryan as the axe severed his leg just under the knee. Blood spurted as he twitched and turned, howling in agony as what was left of the leg hung there, until a second blow detached it completely.

Freed from the guards grasp Myna dropped to her knees pounding the ground with her fists her screams filling the square

However, the executioners were not yet done, blue entrails spurting blood as they slashed at Dryan's body.

"It is enough father!" Suddenly Lyra was before her father, pleading with him to halt the torture. "Kan was my brother, father, as well as your son, but he would not want this...not this.." She pointed a shaking figure towards the dying man as she wept

It was as if Meruk had come out of a trance to face the reality of his command. "Finish it," he ordered Emgot, and a guard drove his spear into the tortured man.

Chapter 3

They were resting by a stream when Jude finally caught up with Incres and those who had chosen to leave, amongst whom were Tomolon and some of his tribe. Incres rose as Jude dismounted from his pony. "What do you think you're doing, Incres? Have you any idea what you're about?" Angrily Jude strode to where those of his tribe were resting.

"You would ask me that Jude, you who are our leader, after what they have done to one of our own?" Incres snarled at him. Here at last was someone upon whom he could vent his anger. "And where would you go? In your pride did you give that a thought? Do you not think that same anger lies in my heart as well as yours? Am I not also of the Maru?"

Incres was unmoved. "You were our leader Jude, and I for one have followed you all my life, even when I judged you to be wrong. I also knew that you had to make decisions that were harsh, and for that I respected you, for a leader must be strong."

"If so, Incres, then you must understand that I have to be strong now. What happened to Dryan was cruel, this I know, but what could I…we have done except to die with him? He should not have stolen the ring. It was that more than anything that made Meruk do what he did. He told me so after he had set you all free. At heart he is a kindly man, Incres, this you must believe."

"Kindly!" Wolf and Myna echoed. Wolf took a step towards his leader.

"Yes, Wolf, for despite the way Dryan died he could do no less to appease Emgot, and those who would follow him, for many loved Meruk's son. It is as you have said, Incres, a leader must be strong and be seen to be strong."

"But did Dryan deserve to die in that way Jude? Was that the action of a kindly man? I think not. "Incres's anger had not cooled, as he faced his leader.

"If you think not, Incres, then who was it that allowed us to settle upon his land- show us how to plant crops so that we may never know hunger- build the stone huts that keep out the winter's chill, and clothe us thus." Jude plucked at his tunic. "Taught you the use of sword and shield so that you may better defend yourself. Even the many words your tongue now speaks were taught by his tribe, so that they no longer look upon us as savages."

"In this you are right, Jude." Tomolon came to join the discourse. "Though I fear it is they who are the savages, for we would never have done to our worst enemies what they have done to one of yours. That is why I now follow Incres wherever that may lead."

As Jude made a gesture of resignation there was a general murmur of approval from the others." And what of those you have left behind? How will they survive without all of you to help them?" Jude scanned those standing or sitting by the stream, for most of the warriors had followed Incres and Tomolon, and a few of the women such as Woona and Myna "You would leave mothers and their mothers behind? Journey to you know not where, to be hunted once again, as it was before Lord Meruk gave us a home?"

Incres read the look of doubt on the faces of some, Jude's words having touched their conscience. He must bring this to an end before some turned back to their home by the lake. "You may live under one whom you believe to be truly kind, Jude; I for one cannot, and I believe I speak for all here. We have said our final farewells to those we have left behind. Perhaps some day when we have found our new home we may meet again."

"And if the gods choose so, Jude, you will also be welcome to make you home with us once again." Wolf's offer came with a mischievous smile.

They all watched as Jude slowly rode away, each with their own thoughts of whether they would see him or their kin again. But to Incres there could be no turning back, for his heart still burned with anger for his friend, and some day he would have his revenge.

They saw the island from the top of the hill. It lay four or more arrow-shots from the shore of the lake.

Wolf scratched his chin. "Are you thinking what I am thinking,

Incres?"

"If I am, my friend, then it will be for the first time," Incres chuckled. "Yes Wolf, I think we see before us a safe haven, that is if we can get across."

"We should build a raft of some sort," Wolf agreed, his eyes still on the island with its waving trees a little way back from the rocky shore.

"A little one to start with I should say," Tomolon suggested. "We do not know the nature of the place. For all we know it may be as barren as my wife's mother." The three men gave a laugh that had Woona and Myna draw closer.

Incres gave them a broad smile, pointing at the island below, before either had a chance to ask what all the laughter was about. "I think we have found our new home."

The women looked in the direction Incres had pointed. "There? "Myna asked with a frown. "Then how are we to get back if we don't decide to bide there? Are we to be prisoners yonder?" Wolf turned up a lip. The girl was right, it might be a place easy to defend, but it could also be a place in which they could be trapped.

Incres believed he knew what his friend was thinking. "First, any enemy must know we are there, then if so, they must build rafts, which we can easily halt before they gain the shore."

"Then we must make sure no one knows we're there, "Tomolon said decisively. "First let's see if we can build a raft, and what yonder island holds for us."

"Well said, my friend," Incres agreed. "Though we shall not find out standing idly here."

They lacked the rope to bind the felled logs together for a larger raft, and the one which they had toiled all day long to build would hold no more than four souls.

"Wolf, Tomolon and Marc will come with me. Emek, "he addressed one of his own tribe, "post guards up yonder on the hill. We'll watch for your signal if you see anyone approaching." At first it seemed that the raft would sink, but gradually, with a little more practice at manoeuvring the awkward craft, somehow, much to the amusement of those on shore, they managed to head it in the direction of the island.

"It's good to hear them laugh, even if it is at our ourselves, "Wolf grinned.

"It's the first time since leaving home, "Tomolon agreed, digging in with his makeshift paddle.

"This is our home now, we have no other. We must never forget that." Incres privately hoped that the island was what he sought.

They pulled up the raft on to a pebble strewn beach, and made their way through trees that almost reached to the waters- edge, emerging into a grassy space dotted here and there with rocks and rotted trees.

"We could build our houses here, Incres," Tomolon exclaimed, kicking happily at a dead tree trunk.

"When we build, Tomolon, it won't be houses, but a settlement with walls higher than three men standing upon one another's shoulders," Incres told them, walking towards the tree line, which was a fair distance away. He estimated that the island was over twenty arrow shots long and about half as wide.

"I saw a boar, and deer as well," Wolf cried excitedly.

Incres knew his friend was eager to show his skill with the bow. "We shall only kill what we need, Wolf. There might not be an abundance of game on an island this small, but we can always hunt on the mainland."

Wolf threw his friend a look of admiration. Now he knew that his decision to follow him had been right

It was well into the evening with the autumn sun sinking over the horizon, the last of its blood red rays reflecting on the still waters of the lake, before almost all were safely across. "What shall we do with the ponies?"

Tomolon asked, for the raft was in no way large enough to accommodate the beasts, and they might well panic on such an unstable vessel. "We must leave them to fend for themselves. We have unburdened them of all the stores we need,"Incres replied sadly.

"Look, it is Marc!" Woona cried as they stood on the shore awaiting the last crossing of their tiny vessel. "He has tied the ponies to the raft and they are swimming behind it!" A cheer went up from those watching on the shore, to subside a little when the ponies appeared to be struggling with the rope in the slight current.

"Will Marc make it, do you think, Wolf?" Myna clutched Wolf's hand anxiously, as she urged on the warrior.

"I think so, he's almost mid-way across and the ponies have ceased to struggle."

At length Marc reached the rocks close to the pebble beach, and men ran into the water to help him.

"Well done, Marc," Incres congratulated the man, while others led the two ponies ashore. "It was nothing, Incres, though I wouldn't like to do it again!" He grinned with pleasure in appreciation of the compliment from the man who was their new leader.

They secured some sort of shelter for the night, and Incres allowed them to hunt on the island this one time. Sitting around a blazing fire which was well hidden from the mainland, Incres set out his plans to the warriors.

"We will build a settlement of wood." Here he halted to point at the surrounding trees. "These we will hack down, thereby making a greater clearing, so that should we be invaded there will be nowhere for our enemies to hide when they attack our settlement."

"How large will this settlement of yours be, Incres? "Wolf asked teasingly, supping at his wine.

"Large enough, friend Wolf for all of us here," Incres responded in good humour.

"All of us Incres?" another asked drawing closer to the fire.

Incres nodded. "And the walls shall be three men high."

Marc let out a low whistle. "That will take a great many trees."

"That will take a great many days!" Wolf guffawed. "That I should live so long."

"That is why we will build it so strong, friend Wolf, so that we may live to curse your grandchildren." At this the meeting broke up in laughter as they went to their makeshift beds.

Next morning Incres took up a stance by the fire. "I can only spare three warriors for the hunting on the mainland," he addressed his men. "Wolf will lead and chose the two others. Try and not be seen if it can be helped. The longer we remain here in secret, the better for us, for though the island is our strength it can also be our weakness." Wolf showed that he understood, as Incres turned to the others. "We must set about building our settlement. Those with axes can start to bring down those trees." He pointed to some trees that stood on the edge of the clearing. "The women and children can fish from the lake. Now let us begin."

Tomolon walked by Incres's side as he started his inspection of the work. "It's a hard task that you've set us, my friend. We will need a great many trees for what you have in mind. Should we not first make shelters so that we may have a little comfort before the hard frost of winter freezes us?"

Incres eyes were firmly fixed upon the trees ahead, as he replied. "No Tomolon, we cannot waste time on that, we must put all our time and effort into building our strong settlement, or we may not survive a greater threat than the frost."

They had almost reached the trees before Incres spoke again, his words intended to reassure the man. "We have only a few warriors to defend us here, and what weapons we have are rightly those of Lord Meruk. Tomorrow I shall have Wolf and a few men make more arrows; these will be our first line of defence."

Tomolon glanced sideways at the man he had chosen to follow. "You are certain we shall be attacked?"

Incres grunted. "It will come some day, we shall not keep our island a secret forever. Besides, hard work will help keep us from dwelling on what has happened to Dryan, and those we have left behind."

The first of the frosts came. They had toiled at building their settlement until only one side remained unfinished. Each day it had taken longer to drag the trees from a greater distance and stand them in the ditch the women and older children had dug.

"The ditch is ready for the trees now, Wolf," Yan cried excitedly, for despite the chill wind the young boy ran with sweat.

"It is well done, Yan, and your sister too has toiled well I see. " Wolf acknowledged the grateful smile of the girl with a wink. Yan frowned. He had expected a little more praise from the man whom he regarded as his hero, even more so than Incres, for Wolf could bring down a dove with the first shot of his arrow.

"You could have given the boy a little more praise, Wolf," Incres panted, helping to stand the huge log in the ditch. "You are his hero after all."

Wolf grinned at his friend. "Naturally. And he will make a fine warrior. He already shows promise with the bow, which is more that I can say of someone a lot older than he."

Incres knew he was making fun of him. "Then perhaps it is I who should hunt on the mainland tomorrow, since it is I who lacks the practice and therefore the skill?" Incres replied tongue in cheek. Wolf was startled, for he loved to hunt, as did all the warriors, in preference to this felling of trees and digging ditches. "You can take Yan with you tomorrow, if you think he is ready." Incres steadied the huge log with his shoulders as the women filled earth and rocks around its base.

"It is almost broken!" Incres suddenly cried at the men on the wooden platform above him. "Why was this not seen to? The ram!" He shouted at them again. The two men there whose job it was to hammer the huge log into the ground stared down at him, so unexpected had come Incres's angry outburst. Incres pointed to the hole with the stake wedged through it near the top, which they used to grip the ram. "If the ram should split, then where will we be? I put you in charge Dorcus, and you have neglected your duties."

The man held out his hands in a gesture of explanation. "It would take another six suns to make another one, Incres. Would you have the men do that instead of this?" He pointed at the ram. "The hole grows larger with wear and I know will soon reach the top, but I believe it will last until the work is done."

"It had better, Dorcus, for all our shelter depends upon our work being done before the first snow falls."

When the log they had manhandled into the ditch had been secured, Incres and Wolf stood back as the ram hammered it into the ground.

"You were hard on him," Wolf said as they walked away.

"Hard? We all have our duties Wolf." Perhaps for the first time the young leader appreciated what Jude must have felt like to be burdened with such responsibilities. "Gista!" Incres crooked a figure at the young girl throwing rocks into the ditch while others wedged them around the logs. She was covered in dirt and mud, the top of her torn wolf skin tunic exposing parts of her tiny breasts. "Help Woona and Myna with the cooking before we all starve," he ordered her gruffly.

"Then you are not all made of stone, are you, friend?" Wolf grinned as he watched the girl happily hurry away. Incres frowned at his friend, though pleased that Wolf did not think him too unfeeling.

Later, on his own, Incres gazed over the dull grey waters of the lake. Most of the tribes-folk were sheltered under the firing platform from where they would fend off any attacker. At present it was crowded, as not all the projected platforms had been built. He himself had chosen to remain outside with Woona in their little shelter, which would appear to others to be an unselfish act by their leader, but which in reality was because he would rather be with her than be crammed with the others under the platform which also acted as a roof. Wolf too remained outside, sometimes with Yan who would come to hear Wolf's stories of their tribe, whilst Myna shared with Gista.

Incres was aware of having changed towards Woona, something of which he was sure she knew, but hoped that in turn she would simply put down to the death of his friend Dryan. Their coupling had become less frequent, and when they did make love, it was Lyra's vision he saw lying beneath him and not that of Woona. What was Meruk's daughter thinking of him now; an accomplice to the slaying of her brother? Would he ever see her again?

The sun was low in the sky when Wolf finally called a halt to that long day's hunting. Yan leaned against a tree. He was near to exhaustion, though he tried not to show it to the rest of the men, especially Wolf. Wolf picked up the three hares he had snared. With the encroaching winter most of the game had gone to ground, and each day they had to travel further inland, which meant that they now had less time to hunt. Fortunately two hunters carried a deer between them; at least they would not go without for some time.

Wolf knew that Incres was worried about the winter. And when he had pointed out that they would not starve, as there was still game on the island, his friend had shown his anger by declaring these should be left to breed, as they would have need of them should they come under siege upon their island.

Wolf signalled that they must keep going, for he did not want to cross the lake in the dark if he could prevent it. The warrior saw how the boy tried to hide his fatigue. "Come on Yan we still have far to travel."

The boy levered himself off the tree and set off behind the others. He wanted so much just to lie down close his eyes and sleep. Perhaps if he just half closed his eyes as he walked it would help. His eyes mere slits Yan staggered behind the others. It was then he missed his footing and slid down the grass banking, hitting a tree stump on the way and landing in amongst a clump of bushes. There was a scream, and at first he was unsure where it had come from. Then there was a rustle in the bushes, and a young girl ran out to be pulled down by a man, and another rose, spear in hand, threatening the boy. An arrow flew through the air and came to rest at the spearman's feet. Startled, the man looked up to where Wolf stood, his warriors by his side.

The strange warrior lowered his spear, and Wolf, followed by the others, ran down the banking as Yan rose to his feet. "There are others amongst the bushes," the boy said, his voice no more than a whisper as he drew closer to his hero.

Wolf aknowledged Yan's warning, his eyes never leaving the face of his adversary.

"Who are you and where have you come from?" Wolf asked, his

bow at the ready.

Wolf's menacing words did not appear to affect the stranger. "I could ask you that same question my strange friend." As the words were leaving his lips other warriors appeared behind him from out of the bushes and nearby trees.

Wolf counted seven of them, against their own four. "We bide a good ways from here," he lied, his thoughts on what Incres would have to say should their island stronghold become known.

The man lowered his spear as though having decided that Wolf and his warriors offered no threat. "We come from the south. The Hunters have chased and killed many of my people. We are all that are left, and wish nothing more than to be left in peace to go our own way."

Wolf heard a baby cry and scanned the bushes where a woman clutched a wailing infant to her breast, while beside her huddled an older child, behind which others stared back at him, their frightened looks reminding him of cornered animals as they crouched there.

"Where will you spend the night?" Wolf asked their leader, for it was clear to him that they could not journey further

The man jerked his head in the direction of the tree lined hill. "We will shelter there, build a fire and hope it is hidden well enough from the Hunters."

"And food?" Wolf asked, aware of so many hungry eyes on the catch which lay up on the banking.

"We will survive somehow, as we have done for the last many suns."

"We can help. We shelter on an island, it is still some distance away and we must hurry before dark. "Beside him Wolf heard the in-drawn breath of the warrior nearest him.

"Incres will be unhappy, Wolf."

Wolf understood the man's concern that Incres wished their presence on the island to remain a secret as long as possible. Now he had told these strangers, and should they not wish to accept his offer, but instead journey on, would they tell others? Or if they did accept, then decide to journey on, would their secret still remain safe? But how could he leave these strangers to their fate, when they looked as his own tribe had done, when they, in turn had been chased for days by these same Hunters?

"We will gladly journey with you to this island of yours, even should it only be until we are rested. We should not wish to burden you with our presence."

Wolf took a step forward, holding out his hands to the frightened woman that he would help carry the child for a time, and so they started for home.

Incres paced back and forth in front of his friend. "Why did you do such a thing Wolf, when you knew I wanted no one to know that we were here on this island?"

Wolf gave his face a little scratch. Mesca had been right in his assumption that their leader would not be happy. "Do you not see something in ourselves, Incres, when you look at them? Are they not as we were when we were hunted by the Hunters?"

Now Incres understood he would never be the leader Jude had been, angry as he was, Wolf was right, he would have done the same. Jude would have hardened his heart and sent them on their way in order to save his own tribe.

"They will have to share the shelters as best they can. You can sleep with Woona and me. Bring Myna, the boy and girl with you. That will give your new friends two shelters at least. Have the other families do the same who live outside the settlement as we do."

Wolf noticed that Incres had said: his new friends, as if holding him responsible for their fate, and perhaps also that of their own tribe.

"You must do something about these strangers, Incres, I cannot stand another night with them." Woona gestured helplessly as Incres stood watching the warriors haul the timber towards the building of the last wall. "They smell." She turned up her nose.

"Did we not also, when we were hunted, and …" he chuckled at the thought, "may still have done had we not met Meruk and his tribe." It was the first time he had said the name aloud, though that man was still in his thoughts each and every day for what he had done to Dryan. "Have them wash in the lake, and if you have it in your heart to be kind, heat some water for them."

"Heat some water!" Woona shrieked at him "What! More work, as if I had not enough to do!" This she knew would not have angered her before, but since Dryan's death Incres had not been the same, and as her anger cooled she bit her lip, for it was plain Incres did not love her any more. Needed her, yes, but love, no? With this still in her mind she turned back to her cooking and the heating of water for these new strangers.

"I fear we offer you some inconvenience." Incres had not heard the man approach. "My name is Matu, I am leader to those who follow me, who do so out of the necessity to survive rather than for my wisdom." The man eyes flickered with amusement while awaiting Incres's reaction. "I shall see that my followers cleanse themselves."

Aware of Incres' embarrassment, Matu pointed to the men hoisting another great log into place on the wall. "I have never seen such high walls, even the Lord Meruk has nothing to compare with that. It must have taken many suns to raise such a place."

At the mention of his enemy, Incres swung upon the man. "You know of this man? You have seen his settlement?"

Taken aback by the brusqueness of the question, Matu caught his breath before answering.

"I have. He is a wise and good man. But I have not set eyes upon him for many seasons, though I hear he still lives. Some travellers told me that he has lost his only son. Murdered some would have it. I should not wish to be the one who would have done such a deed if he is caught by Meruk, should this be so." He was aware of Incres's face having darkened while he spoke. Why do you ask of the man? Do you also know of him?"

"I do, " Incres seethed. "It was he who tortured my friend for that same death. But there was no murder." Incres swung angrily on his heel and walked swiftly to the new settlement wall.

At last the settlement was complete, now all their time and effort could be focused on the hunting. Having travelled for almost half of the day, Incres called a halt in a wooded clearing high on the hills. "We'll split up here, and return with whatever game we can find. Watch for the sun sinking beyond the hill yonder. It will be a slower journey back carrying our kill, should fortune favour us and we must not get caught here in the dark."

Incres watched as the small bands of men disappeared amongst the trees. They totalled twenty five warriors, none having been left behind to guard the island. "We must make this a good hunt, Wolf, snow is not so many days away. Game will have gone deeper and higher into the forest, and we shall not be able to journey much further than this in a day."

"When the snow comes we can follow their tracks," Wolf suggested.

"So can the Hunters. Would you have them follow our tracks back to the island?"

"No, I suppose not." Wolf grinned at his own folly.

It was dusk when the last hunting party finally returned to the clearing.

"I have sent some men on, who have returned earlier," Incres explained. "Your party, Matu, are the last."

The tall, slim man slid down on to a tree stump. "We did not find much."

Incres nodded his understanding, acknowledging that these men whom Wolf had found were still weak from their earlier pursuit by The Hunters. "You have no time to rest, Matu, if you and your warriors are to reach the island before dark."

It seemed to take all of the man's strength to get to his feet. "We shall not let you down, Incres,"he said firmly, and gestured to his little band of men to take up their catch.

The two bands had almost reached the foot of the hill when Incres saw a figure he did not recognise vanish amongst the trees a little way to his right. At first he took it to be one of the bands he had already sent ahead, when he heard a cry of alarm, and a fleeing man appeared from out of the trees to head in their direction.

"A Hunter!" Matu gasped, and before the man's words had left his lips, Incres was running full tilt at the approaching man. This man must not get away, was all Incres could think off as he ran, or the island would no longer be

their sanctuary. It was as he raised his spear that he saw the man crumple with an arrow in his chest. Panting, Incres swivelled around to see an exultant Wolf trot up beside him. Incres barked angrily at him. "There could be more of them, dolt!." Did Wolf never understand the seriousness of situations such as this? Then, as he started to run past the dead man to where a band of his own warriors were emerging out of the trees, his thoughts were that Wolf never would understand. "Are there more of them, Tomolon?" Incres gasped at the man, while taking a hasty look around.

"We saw only one, but The Hunters do not travel alone. Should we search for more, Incres do you think?"

Incres thought for a moment. If they took time to search for more of their dreaded enemy they would not reach the island before nightfall. How many eyes were watching them right now he thought? Resigned to the fact that their island was no longer a secret, Incres turned his face homeward.

Incres was relieved that they had completed their stronghold, nor did he fear an attack from the Hunters now that winter snow was already on the hills. Not when these same attackers would have to take time to build rafts, gauge their numbers, as well as feed themselves. No, he decided they would be safe until the warmer weather.

The young leader made a decision. They must store more food to see them through the long cold days. And if so, it must be done now, while those of The Hunters who may have seen them yesterday were on their way back to tell their leader Arcana. He had to consider that they might have been seen in the first place, and if so had the Hunters left some of their number behind to watch their coming and going from the island?

Next day Incres summoned Tomolon to him. "I shall leave you in charge here, Tomolon with a few men to continue the task of building the remainder of our firing platforms."

"You mean to hunt again today Incres?" The man raised his eyebrows in surprise.

"We must, before the Hunters return. They will not attack the island, though they might try to prevent us from leaving, or wait until we do, then hope to surprise us in the woods. Today we will journey in the opposite direction to yesterday, and hunt in the woods on the hills there. Let us hope no eyes will watch what we do."

"It's a good plan, Incres. If any of the Hunters await your return to where you hunted yesterday they will find it a long cold wait," the man laughed.

Incres moved away. "I hope you're right, Tomolon". He hesitated for a moment, then turned to face the man. "Should I not return, you must become leader here." At the man's gasp of surprise, explained, "Wolf is too…"

Tomolon nodded his understanding.

"Have no fear, Incres my friend, somehow that little problem will not arise today, you will be back by the fire's light this night."

"I have seen nothing all day except this, Incres." Wolf kicked at the hare at his feet. "Let us hope the other parties have fared better."

Despite the disappointment of the day's hunting, Incres could not resist teasing his friend. "Not much for an expert bowman such as yourself, Wolf?" He gave the fox that he himself had killed with his spear, a nudge with his foot.

Wolf recognised what he knew to be a jibe at his expense. "The day is not yet spent," he said loftily.

Incres stepped closer to his fellow tribesman. "Beyond the bushes yonder, do you see them?" he whispered. Wolf swept the bushes with an eye, expecting to see some animal lurking there, instead what he saw were three men walking stealthily uphill away from where he and Incres stood.

"They haven't seen us in this fading light, Incres -Hunters no doubt."

"Let's step back into the bushes behind us; if we're not seen so much the better." Incres's words had scarcely left his lips when he heard the sound of one of his own parties returning, instantly alerting the three Hunter who spun round. Wolf's arrow took the first Hunter by surprise, and before the other two knew where it had come from,his next arrow felled a second.

Incres ran. He had to halt the third man from getting away. The lone survivor saw him and to Incres' surprise halted and threw down his spear in a token of submission. Close behind him he could hear Wolf's heavy breathing, then suddenly his own returning party were with him.

He took a step towards the man. "You are of the Hunters?" he asked, his voice sharp.

The man gave a little choke as he nodded. "I am with the Hunters, though I am not one of them."

"But you hunt and kill as though one of them." The frightened man gave another nod. "So why are you here? Is not your land further south?"

"It is Lord Arcana's wish that we kill all who pass this way."

Incres was well aware of the ways of the Hunters. It was not only for their few possessions that the poor were hunted, but to demonstrate the power of Arcana. This too had been the reason for their pursuing his own tribe and the subsequent death of his mother and many more. He remembered Jude telling him that by pursuing and killing all the smaller tribes it was Arcana's way of ensuring that these same small tribes could not band together and perhaps some day become a threat to his power.

"We must kill him, Incres." Dorcus raised his spear, awaiting his leader's command, his eyes glaring at the trembling man.

"I have a woman and two children," the frightened man pleaded. "It is not by choice that I hunt with this tribe." The man pulled up his sleeve to reveal the symbol of a spear burned into his arm. "When the Hunters find a broken tribe, instead of killing the warriors such as myself they take our women and children and force us to do their bidding. If we do not…"

Incres gently lowered Dorcus's spear, understanding what the man had left unsaid. In this way Arcana grew even more powerful.

"Where are the Hunters now?" he asked.

"Lord Arcana is still in his settlement in the south, but he has sent parties such as this one as far north as this. We are to return with the first of the snows. We have already sent him many warriors…"

Anxious to know whether he or the Hunters knew of their island, Incres asked with a wave of his hand, "How long have you hunted here?"

"Nine …ten suns."

"You know from where we came?" The man shook his head, and Incres searched his face for any sign that he might be lying. Satisfied that he was not, he studied the ground at his feet. What to do next was the question. Should he let him go, back to his woman and children in the hope he would not tell his lord of their meeting? Or instead kill him and ensure their safety on the island, at least until the winter was over? In his heart he knew what Jude would have done. The survival of the tribe must come first, but he was not Jude. Had the Hunters caught warriors of his own tribe would they have done what this man was forced to do to save those of their own?

Wolf caught the troubled expression on Incres's face. "You will send him on his way?" "Will you swear to tell no one…not even your woman, of your finding us, if I let you go?" Incres asked the man, having decided what to do.

The man's face lit up, a chance to live was open to him by the way this leader had spoken.

"You have my word…?"

Incres waved aside the obvious question, for it was better than no one should know his name or tribe.

"Go. Tell no one."

The grateful man had hurriedly disappeared into the woods and they were on their way, before Wolf spoke. "I think it is a mistake you may…we," he corrected himself, " may live to regret."

"I think not, Wolf," Mesca said, pointing back to where Dorcus was running to catch up.

Incres swivelled round, his grip tightening on his spear, waiting until a panting, smiling Dorcus drew up before them, and in one swift movement, Incres' spear had taken him in the throat. As the stricken man slid to the ground his face now a mixture of surprise and disbelief, Incres faced the astonished band. "Did I not command that the man should be free to go? I will not have my command disobeyed. Do you all understand?" As much shaken as the others,

Wolf stared in disbelief, for he had never seen or heard his friend so angry in all of their years together. Incres angrily scanned the tiny band of men. "If we are to survive at all, there must be only one leader and his word, law.

Now let us go home."

They saw no other enemy that day or the next. Finally, the snows came and they could no longer hunt. The island was their fortress and their prison.

The days passed quickly for a people busy completing their new homes. At ground level underneath the firing platforms the families had made their homes, some having built another storey directly beneath the platforms which could be reached by means of ladders and which could be used as sleeping quarters.

The nights however were a different matter. As leader, Incres shared one of these dwellings with Woona, while both Gista and Yan dwelt with Wolf, and Myna

"Do you think Wolf will couple with Myna?" Woona asked as they snuggled up together a coverlet of wolf skins.

At first Incres did not stir: his thoughts were far away at the Asan settlement where so much had happened to affect his life. His coupling with Lyra, the brutal death of Dryan, both were never far from his thoughts. That he would never see his friend again, this he understood. But Lyra?

"Incres, are you asleep?" Woona tugged at his upper arm

"Not now, you restless woman," Incres scolded her. Woona drew him closer, tonight she would make their coupling better than ever before. She would not lose this warrior of hers to a ghost.

They fear me, were Incres's thoughts as he oversaw the gate being slid into place between two of the stoutest trees they could find. The gate itself was no more than a barrier, a spears length wide, behind which lay another in readiness if and when the time came: for desperate defence and come it would, of this Incres had no doubt. The inner gate would act as a second, more robust, barrier.

"All is complete, Incres, it took longer without..." Cursing himself for a fool, Tomolon bit his lip.

"Without Dorcus, you were about to say?" Incres finished the sentence for him.

"Well yes, if you must know," the man said defiantly.

"You think I was wrong to slay the man? Tell me the truth, Tomolon, for I value your thoughts."

Tomolon pretended to study the gate as he answered. "All followed you out of respect and in some ways for your wisdom. Now they follow out of the sheer necessity to survive. Expect no more."

"You believe they hate me? Or is it fear that I see in their eyes when I pass?"

"With some it is both, especially those of your own tribe, and more so Dorcus's own brother, Briunic. That is someone you should watch." Incres's expression did not change as the man spoke, though his heart missed a beat or two. Did he not have enough to think about without the added worry of having a spear in the back?

He had faced Briunic when man had confronted him regarding the slaying of his brother. Even as he tried to explain his reasons for doing so, he saw the hatred and anger in the man's eyes. His slaying of Dorcus had been in anger, an anger that he had been disobeyed as leader, something Dorcus would not have done had Jude still led. But also because Dorcus had put the tribe at risk. For although the man had mistakenly thought that by killing the Hunter he had kept their island a secret, he had in fact done the very opposite. With several of their number missing the Hunters were sure to search for them, which is why he had left that unfortunate man unburied as he had done with Dorcus, in the hope that should the Hunters find them they would conclude that they had slain one another. He hoped that by doing so, Arcana would not vent his wrath upon the man's family, if he'd thought that he had deserted.

"You've done something Jude would never have done however angry or hard pressed he may have been," Tomolon was saying. "So think upon what my people must see in you, you who have slain one of your own."

Jude…Jude, must he always live in the shadow of that man? But Jude had not brought them here, had them build a fortress in order to survive. This is what it was all about, survival, and if they did not understand this, then his slaying of Dorcus would have been for nothing.

"You mean to hunt again today?" Tomolon changed the delicate subject, as Incres shouldered his bow."

"Today will be our last I fear, Tomolon. The snow is not so very far away, then we shall have to snare our game when they come to drink by the water's edge at night."

"We still have game here on our island."

"No, Tomolon, as I have said before, the beasts here must be our last resort, let them breed for our own purpose. We may yet have need of all of them."

They had reached the water's edge before Incres spoke again. "While we're gone, I will leave you with a task that I lack the courage to do myself" Tomolon drew up as the hunting party hauled the raft into the water. "I want you to teach the women the use of the bow." Incres heard Wolf laugh, and swung around. "You think this a laughing matter Wolf? Perhaps, as you regard yourself master of that weapon you would rather stay behind yourself?

Wolf held up his hands in a gesture of surrender. "I don't have that kind of courage either!" he laughed, and the others joined in.

"It has never been done before, Incres. The women will hate you for it, especially my woman, as she could not hit a side of the settlement even if she were to stand a spear length from it,." Emek chuckled with a shake of his head.

"Then Tomolon will teach her, Emek," Incres snarled at him. And the party grew silent, for this man whom they had thought they had known would now brook no disobedience.

For the past four nights Wolf and his party had lain in wait for the animals coming to drink by the water's edge. Now the raft headed back to the island.

Balancing with difficulty on the tiny craft, Emek gave a little shiver in the frosty evening.

"The game grow scarcer every night, Wolf."

Woolf gave a nod. "Most have gone to sleep until the sun warms Mother earth again. Would that we had that same sense."

Emek was right in thinking, that there was little to be gained from lying in wait to freeze in the cold night air, while the moon cast eerie shadows across the water. However he would be wrong to think that Incres would not continue to send other parties across each night.

It was Tomolon who eventually came to their rescue. "The night parties return almost empty handed, Incres; each night they bring back less and less."

"Do we have enough in the stone house to see us through until it is warm again?" Incres' voice had an edge to it as he asked the question.

"I believe so. However, if all else fails, there is always the animals here, for unlike their brothers and sisters on the mainland they are trapped." Tomolon held up his hands, as if he had anticipated his leader's answer. "I know you want the animals here to multiply, for it would seem that you are certain that some day we will find ourselves besieged, but better this than see little children starve."

"If that's what you think, Tomolon, it is as well that it is I and not you who leads here."

The unexpected rebuke stung the older man. "I was leader of my own tribe for many a day. Or have you forgotten this in the midst of that anger which seems to eat deeper into your heart with each passing day?"

It was the other man's turn to start. Was it so plain, Incres wondered? Was it in fact anger? If so, at what? Was it indeed all about how Dryan had died? Or that he himself had slain a good man; a thought that continually nagged at his very soul? Each day it had not grown easier, as he believed it would have done as he became more accustomed to leadership. His only consolation, he well knew, was when he thought of Lyra, and the hope of seeing her again. And should this be ever so, would she forgive him and the part he had played in the death of her brother? Perhaps he had been too harsh on Tomolon, but he must show strength. "If that is all you wish to say, my friend Tomolon, then I have other matters to attend to."

"No, I have more that must be said." Tomolon drew himself up to his full height. "You send hunting parties across to the mainland where they lie in wait for game. Have you seen them upon their return, their fingers so stiff with cold that they are scarcely able to grip an oar? And for what? All the animals have gone to ground until Mother Earth awakens again."

"There is a fire awaiting their return. What more do they want?" Incres answered, annoyed by this stubborn man's questions.

Tomolon gave a mocking laugh. "A fire you say? A fire no doubt outside in the open? There are none in our homes and we freeze at night, despite the wolf skins we pile on top of us." "Would you have me allow them a fire in their huts when you know all are made of wood? Would you see the settlement which we have worked so long and hard to build destroyed by one careless spark? Is this what you seek Tomolon my friend?" Incres seethed at the man.

"It need not be so. The ground in their huts is not made of wood, they could dig a pit there as we have done in our own tribe. I can show you how to make a fire from wood that is slow to burn and with little smoke. And what little there is will find its way through the slits in the platforms above."

Though reluctant to cool his anger, Incres stopped to think. It was a good plan, and he had to admit to being cold despite the hot stones he and others took from the fire each night in an attempt to heat their huts.

Swallowing his anger as well as his pride, Incres used a more conciliatory tone. "You can do this without danger of burning what we have built?"

Tomolon nodded. "This I can do. And it will go well to help keep their spirits up."

Once again Incres was on his guard. "The tasks which I mean to set them will keep them warm enough, Tomolon. However, you may try this plan of yours in my hut come tomorrow."

Wolf strode happily across the settlement square. At last Incres had seen sense and halted the night hunting parties, and with Tomolon's help they now had a fire in each hut to keep themselves warm. What was this meeting about, he wondered, that Incres had commanded him and a few others to attend?

Wary, Wolf approached the fire in the centre of the settlement where others were already assembled.

"You slept well I hope, Wolf?" Incres asked sarcastically. "I thought you too had gone to sleep like our furry friends."

Wolf gave a wide grin, he would not let his friend annoy him, not today, not after his coupling with Myna. He remembered his surprise at her coming to him in the night, putting her finger to her lips and taking his hand and leading him down the wooden ladder from where they both had lain beside Gista and Yan. There, she had lain down by the fire inviting him to take her, make love. He had felt uncomfortable with the children so close above, but she had put him at ease by silently drawing down her covering, leaving him to drink in her nakedness and he knew he could not resist his mounting desire for her.

Incres drew a sketch of the island in the soft snow. "This is where we land the rafts." He pointed with his stick to where they had originally landed. "And here at the top of our island is the only other landing place. It is here we will build a shelter for those I mean to have stand guard when the time comes. We cannot send a signal back if attackers were to land there as it would be hidden by the trees, so whoever stands guard will take a pony with him."

He halted to look at each in turn as if challenging any to contradict him; when all remained silent, he continued. "I do not expect any attack at least until the weather warms, so this will give us time to be better prepared when it does."

"You are certain of this attack you speak so much about, Incres?" Matu ventured to ask, glancing across to where Wolf stood, in the hope the younger man would support him

"Do you think we will keep this island of ours secret for ever, Matu?" Incres asked sharply. He pointed above him. "We cannot hide all the smoke from our fires."

"Perhaps not, but whoever might come here with evil in his heart must first cross the lake," Matu answered determined not to be browbeaten.

"Yes, Matu, and it is there we must halt them, before they land. This is why you, Wolf, will have men make arrows, as many as there are trees on the island. You Arno, will set men to work in the making of spears, as many as Wolf has arrows."

The men looked at one another, and it was Wolf who finally spoke. "It is a good plan, Incres my friend, and should this attack come as you say it will, we shall need as many of these weapons as we can craft."

For once Incres acknowledged a comment with a glimmer of appreciation. "I'm glad it meets with your approval, Wolf," he grinned

Tomolon drew closer to the fire. "When the weather becomes kinder again and we can hunt on the mainland, it will be then that we must be most on the alert."

"You are right, my friend," Incres nodded. "It is as Tomolon says, it is then we must be most careful. But first things first; let us make a start to the making of our weapons. And you Marco, instead of Emek, can teach the women the art of firing the bow, eh?. "He laughed as he stood up. It was the first time since coming to the island that they could remember their leader having laughed.

For the remainder of that first winter on the island, the tribes set about improving their fortress- making weapons, learning to wield swords, use bows and arrows as well as the daily tasks.

At last the snow melted. Mother Earth awoke and came to life, and they set about clearing the land ready for planting seeds, the first of their new home.

Marc and Arno strode across the square to where Incres stood talking to Woona and Myna, then sensing that they had something important to discuss, Incres left the women to face the warriors.

"You look as though you have some trouble on your minds, friends," Incres asked, a flicker of a smile on his lips.

"We have, Incres." Marc looked his leader in the eye. "I …we," he corrected himself, "talked over the fire last night." Again he halted as Incres raised an eyebrow. "It was only by chance that we discussed our kin back by the caves at the lake, you understand." Once more Marc halted as if afraid that Incres might see some hint of treachery in their meeting.

Arno brushed Marc's hesitancy aside. "We should like to return to the caves to see our kin again and find out, now that we have found a new home, if they should wish to return with us."

"We miss them Incres," Marc said in support of his friend.

Although he had no near kin to him now that his mother was dead, Incres could well understand the feelings of the warriors. And of how many more, he wondered?

"They are old…most of them, and may not survive such a journey, it is more than five sunrises distant, should they wish to return with us" Incres demurred.

"We could make light of the journey by taking it gently?" Arno suggested, sensing a glimmer of hope by the way his leader had spoken.

"If you do, and you are found by the Hunters, what then my friends?" Incres asked of the men, his words now hard.

Arno was not to be dissuaded, he for one was anxious to find out what had befallen his mother and a sister who could not be persuaded to leave with him. He himself should have stayed behind, but they had insisted on his leaving with Incres.

"If you say that we must not leave, Incres, you may wake up one morning to find all of the Maru have gone."

"Is that a threat, Arno?"

The warrior studied his feet. "No, Incres, it is a fact. What will be left for you to command if all of us are gone? Perhaps we may all return with Jude as our leader?" Arno realised his mistake as soon as the words had left his lips, for Incres face had clouded with rage. Then to his amazement and relief his leader's countenance gradually softened as if he had digested what had been said.

"If this is your wish, then who am I to prevent you. Perhaps there is something in what you say, that you might be able to bring back those who wish to find a safe shelter here on the island. Yes, Arno my friend, it is a good idea. We will start two suns from now, and I shall come with you."

As the bewildered men walked away, Incres smiled to himself, for they had unwittingly given him the opportunity of seeing Lyra again.

The sun shone across the lake by the caves as if welcoming home its lost souls. When in sight of the stone huts which they had left all those suns and moons before, the warriors started to run, some calling out the names of those loved ones left behind.

Shading his eyes with a hand against the early Spring sun, Jude awaited their approach.

"You have seen the wisdom of returning home, Incres?" Jude asked in welcome, his eyes shining at this unexpected sight.

"No, Jude, we have come to take you home."

Jude's expression changed to one of disappointment. "We do well here under the Lord Meruk." To emphasis the point he threw out a hand to encompass the planted corn.

"You have done well as you say, Jude," Incres conceded, "but we too raise crops, except that what we grow is our own."

"Perhaps so, Incres, but it would not have been so if the Lord Meruk had not given you that same seed and shown you how it was done," Jude reminded the stubborn young man.

"I did not come to quarrel with you, Jude. There is a place for you and all who might wish to return with us. However, if you do not wish to join us, there is one favour that I would ask of you in the name of the safety of our tribe , and that is that you tell no one of the whereabouts of our new home."

If Jude was insulted by the request, he gave no sign. "The safety of the Maru has always been my first concern, this you must have learned by this time. If not, you are no leader, Incres my friend."

Incres coloured. That he had insulted one whom he had so admired was clear. "I take back my words, Jude, I had no wish to offend you."

Jude stepped forward and put an arm around the young warrior's shoulders. "We will say no more about it. Come, let us eat."

On the journey Incres had thought up a plan in which he could leave the camp by the caves and journey to see Lyra; a plan which seemed to him both reasonable and feasible. Seven days later they started their journey back. Only a few, such as Marc's mother and sister, had come with them, the remainder of the Maru having elected to stay under the protection of the Lord Meruk.

For some reason Incres felt guilty at what he had done, though he saw it as the only means of preserving the tribe. He had left Jude behind with all that remained; mainly the old and the sick, with only a few warriors left to hunt and sew the crops.

Later that day, mounted on one of the ponies, Incres left the others with the excuse, mainly to Woona who had accompanied him, that he would scout out the land to ensure no Hunters were in the vicinity and also to find any game, when in fact his intention was to ride to the settlement of the Asan to seek out Lyra. How he was to find her without being seen he had not yet worked out.

A slight breeze drifted over the river where Incres had first seen Lyra draw water. It was after noon, perhaps he was too late to see her. A woman appeared through the gate of the settlement, and for a moment, Incres heart leaped, thinking that it might be Lyra, only to find that it was not. A few minutes later another made her way to the water's edge and instinctively Incres drew back into his hiding place behind a screen of bushes. Perhaps, he wondered, Lyra no longer went to the river for water? Or if she did, he thought, perhaps only in the early morning? And if he were not to return to his tribe until tomorrow, what excuse could he give for his absence, especially to Woona?

Incres' mind went over and over what he must do if he stayed here. He could not return empty handed. Could he put the blame on his mount, it having become lame or some such excuse? He turned a little to see if the pony could be seen from where he lay. If it should be discovered he would be in trouble in more ways than one.

It was as these thoughts coursed through his mind that he saw her. He sat up abruptly, unsure if his eyes had deceived him. No, they had not, it was her, but unfortunately in the company of another two women.

Incres rose and stealthily made his way behind what cover he could find to towards where the three women had halted by the river. Darting a quick glance at the settlement to make sure that no guards were watching, he ran for the cover of a large rock within earshot of the water-carriers, and crouched down waiting.

One of the women waded a little way into the water to wash herself while those on the banking watched and laughed at something she was saying. Incres's breath came in short gasps, Lyra, her back to him, was only a short stone's-throw away standing a little way behind the others. Lifting a small stone, he threw it at her, hitting her gently on the back. Giving a little gasp the girl turned round and as she did so, Incres waved at her from his hiding place. For a moment Lyra stood there staring as if disbelieving at who she was seeing, until Incres waved again. Lyra turned back to the river and Incres heart sank, that she had seen him he had no doubt, but of her wanting to speak to him he was unsure.

Suddenly all sorts of doubts flooded Incres's mind. Was it that she did not want to speak to someone who, however indirectly, had been party to the death of her brother? Or to someone who had shown their ingratitude to her father for all he had done to help the Maru by leading most of his tribe away? Incres drew back against the rock. He should not have come. Lyra no longer wished to know him.

Sad at the prospect that this must be so, Incres sat there, waiting until the sun sank behind the hills when it would be dark enough for him to leave unseen. That he would return to his band without having caught any game troubled him less than not having spoken to the lovely creature who he had come to love, albeit in his dreams and imagination.

He heard women talking again, this time closer, and he drew back into the rock, as they passed close by on their way to the settlement. Only when they had passed did he notice that Lyra was not one of them. A little distance on, one woman halted to hitch at her basket of washing as she turned to call out to Lyra that she must hurry.

Peering round the other side of his hiding place Incres saw Lyra make a sign that she intended to relieve herself behind his rock. His heart pounding, Incres could scarcely wait. As the girl rounded his hiding place he pulled her down and before she knew it, he had smothered her with kisses, telling her as he did so how much he had missed her.

Almost roughly Lyra pushed back the zealous warrior. "Incres, what are you doing here? I thought you had taken the Maru many suns away?" She gasped for breath.

"It is not all that many suns away. Lyra, will you come with me, it is a safe place where we have chosen to dwell?"

Lyra drew back as if what he had said had been a fantasy. "To where Incres? And to what?"

For a moment Incres was about to tell her of their island, but remembered how he had made all others keep their secret. "Does it matter? We will be together."

"Incres, have you forgotten that I am the daughter of Lord Meruk, leader of the Asan?" she said haughtily. "Would you have me betray that trust by having me live with those who have helped slay my brother?"

"None of the Maru wanted your brother's death, he was not slain out of malice or revenge...it was an accident," Incres said angrily. "And have we not all paid the price through the death of my friend Dryan? Do you seek more? Has your father's soul not rested, now that he has had his revenge? I will ask you again Lyra, come away with me to a new life, for I love you dearly."

"I will not break my father's heart further, Incres. You must leave me to the life that I must live as the daughter of Lord Meruk." Lyra rose, her hand on the rock.

"The thought that I will never see you again Lyra, will surely break my heart, for I have thought of little else since last we met."

Incres rose and took her hand but Lyra cast a hasty glance to the settlement wall. "You must go now. The women whom I came here with will come in search of me," she said anxiously. "Go, Incres and may the Gods go with you."

It was almost dark, and as Incres rode his pony at a trot he saw a mounted figure coming towards him, and when still some distance away recognised the rider as Wolf, a deer slung across his pony's neck.

"So, your meeting went well?" Wolf drew up the panting beast, an amused look upon his face as he asked the question. "Oh, I well knew where you were headed when you took yourself off hunting." Wolf's grin broadened at his friend discomfiture.

"She wouldn't come, Wolf," Incres replied sadly.

Wolf swung his pony closer. "Here. "He lifted the deer and threw it across Incres's mount. "It will help keep Woona from asking awkward questions."

It was Wolf's mention of the name that had Incres thinking he had not given Woona a thought all that long disastrous day, and of the consequences had Lyra decided to return with him.

Chapter 4

On such a warm day it was difficult not to be happy. Incres watched his hunters as they climbed the slope, Yan well to the fore, laughing and urging on the gasping warriors.

It was surprising how the boy had grown over the cold sunless time. That Wolf was still his hero was not difficult to see, the way he copied everything that man did.

"I wish I had his energy, Incres," Marc panted beside him. "He is almost a man grown and can fire an arrow as well as the best of us."

"Or the worst," Incres laughed at himself.

Marc pointed up the slope to where Wolf stood with the boy. "I think they want you to see something, Incres."

Yan waited impatiently for Incres to reach the top. "There! "The boy pointed excitedly to a large settlement at the foot of a valley. "What tribe are they, Incres? Do you know?"

Instead of answering, Incres started down the hill.

"Shouldn't we wait, and see what they are about? "Arno voiced his concern as he stumbled after his leader.

"What they are about isn't too difficult to see, Arno. They are about their own business, and should they have had the notion to harm us, would have done so many strides back when they first saw us." Arno threw his leader a sideways glance. "Their warriors have followed us since we crossed that stream back yonder. It grieves me to be leading so may blind men, Arno." Incres gave an artificial sigh.

Incres led his men down the hill, where he drew them to a halt at the open gate.

"Bide here, Wolf, I shall greet them alone." He handed his friend his spear and started through the gate.

Almost at once a tall elderly man emerged from a hut, and Incres raised his hand in a friendly salute. "I am Incres, leader of the Maru," he said pleasantly. "I wish you no harm." The elderly man with the flowing white hair walked quietly forward as those around halted in their work to gaze at this strangely dressed visitor. "I am Trebac, leader of the Louma tribe, and I bid you welcome, friend," he answered kindly. And instantly Incres warmed to the man.

"I have warriors back yonder. "Incres jerked his head to where Wolf and the rest stood waiting.

"They too are welcome to our home," the leader replied. Their new friend set Incres down to fare he had not seen in many a day, while his fellow tribesmen sat outside in the open, eating, drinking and chatting with the denizens.

"You have travelled far friend? Trebac asked politely as he munched on his meat.

"A few sunrises."

His host gave a little chuckle as if savouring some unknown jest. "You are from the south. I can see that by the way you describe each day as sunrises." Incres blushed. It was the old way his tribe had of describing a day.

"I see I have offended you, my friend. Believe me it was not intended. It is only we of the tribes that are not from the south speak and see things differently."

Feeling better for the pleasant apology, Incres gave a nod. "Then I will tell you something that you do not know." Incres gestured with the joint of meat that he had been chewing. "The Hunters will find this place and destroy it. They too, are from the south, but as the days…" he paused to smile at the man, "grow warmer they will journey north".

It was the first time Trebac had shown concern. "How come you by this news?"

In some detail Incres told him of their unexpected encounter with the warrior that Dorcus had slain, and how the Hunters forced the warriors they had captured into hunting and raiding for them, for fear of having their families killed. When he had finished he felt an inward pride at having a knowledge that this man did not have.

"I shall have my warriors scout far and wide for any sign of these people." Trebac sat back, his eyes focused beyond the walls of the wooden hut. "I thank you for this, my friend."

Incres stood up. "We have far to travel before this day is done."

"Very well, if you must leave, so be it." Trebac too rose, and as they emerged into the sunlight Yan came running to them crying excitedly

"Incres! Incres! these people have corn as we do on our island!" The boy saw the anger on his leader's face as he drew to an abrupt halt at having said the unforgivable.

If Trebac understood he made no sign, except to ask, "This surprises you, young one? Is it not so in the savage south?" His laughter was intended to preclude any thought of an insult. "We were shown how it is done by the Asan before we became our own men again," Incres quickly explained.

"Meruk their leader is a good, though powerful man I understand," Trebac commented as they walked towards the gate, Wolf and the others close behind.

Incres held his peace. "So I believe."

Here their host believed it prudent to leave it there.

Yan trailed behind as the men made their way back to the island. That he had disgraced himself in front of everyone he had no doubt. What Incres would do or say to him worried him, but not as much as what Wolf would think of him now.

Yan's hero watched the boy, head down, dragging his feet as though they weighed the earth.

"He is ashamed of what he said back yonder, Incres. Do not be too hard on him, he is still only a child."

Incres looked back down the hill to where the boy, usually the first to any top, halted now and again to kick angrily at the grass.

"We were younger than he, Wolf, when we learned our first lesson of what our ill actions could cost the rest of the tribe."

Wolf had known Incres since they were boys. Then, he was brave, in some ways gentle, but now Wolf was unsure if much of the latter remained. What punishment would he mete out to the boy for betraying their hiding place? Wolf gripped his spear tighter, remembering what Incres had done to Dorcus. No, he would not let him harm him…at least not beyond what punishment he deserved.

"I'm surprised that our island has not been discovered before, Wolf. The boy will have learned a lesson. I believe allowing him to fret a little will be punishment enough. Besides," he smiled at his friend. "Is this not a good and sunny day? Come on, Wolf, let's walk together and I shall teach you the words that mean summer and winter."

It was hot for an autumn day . Incres waved down the slope to where Woona and the women worked. Woona waved back, holding up the flowers she had gathered. He had made their day by allowing them to cross to the mainland, where some like Woona gathered flowers, while others searched for the teeth of dead wolves and other animals with which to decorate themselves.

They had crossed from the small landing-place at the head of the island where the new watch-tower stood. It had taken some time to build, this, and the three rafts which they would keep there.

There had also been the hard work of clearing the land to plant their crops. Incres had chosen land a little way from the settlement, which he had hoped would be the easiest to clear, but this had not been so, as each turn of their tools had hit upon stone or roots of the trees they had felled for the building of the settlement. But at last it was done, though the corn was not as high as that which he had seen at the settlement of the white haired Trebec. Maybe next year would see it improve, he thought.

No sooner had these thoughts left his mind when he heard a shout. Looking up from whence it came it was to see an agitated Wolf waving at him and thrusting his spear in the direction of the island. Incres swung round. There, some distance away came a running, straggling column of men, with women clutching children to them, all, it would appear, in a state of panic.

Wolf slithered to his side. "Can you make out who they are, Incres?" He put a hand up to shade his eyes from the sun.

Incres shook his head. I've no idea. But whoever they are, they're being chased by someone, and if it's the Hunters, they are too close to our island."

"I recognise that man!" Wolf cried, taking his hand away from his eyes. "It's Trebac! I'd know that mane of snow-white hair anywhere!"

Incres had already started down the slope, calling out to the women that they must hurry back to the rafts.

Coming from the side of the hill, Arno ran beside him. "What shall we do, Incres, they'll surely see us crossing to the island?" the man gasped. "If it is the Hunters who are chasing them our island will no longer be a secret!"

Incres was only too well aware of this, but why had Trebac led his tribe here? Why had he not remained to defend his settlement? He ushered the women quickly onto the rafts.

"You men, when you've landed the women on shore, return here as swiftly as you can," he ordered the warriors, who had already started to row. "Yan!" he called out to the boy. "On to a raft with you now, and when you reach the other side ride the pony to the settlement and alert the tribe as to what is happening here. Do not fail me, boy."

A beam of pride lit the boy's face at being given such an important task. "I won't let you down, Incres," he shouted leaping on to one of the moving rafts.

Incres ran to meet Trebac, who was stopping now and again to urge on the stragglers to greater speed.

"Trebac, how come you to be here?" he shouted, darting a quick glance behind the old man to see if any pursuers were in sight.

"The Hunters are after us, Incres, and your island is our only hope of safety," the old man panted, his white hair flowing in the breeze so that he stood there like some god that Incres had once seen set in stone.

"Why did you not bide to defend your homes, and all that you have laboured to make your own?"

The old man looked anxiously behind him, before replying. "My scouts told me they were too many for us. This, and what you told me about their enslaving warriors to fight for them in fear of having their loved ones slaughtered, left me with nothing other than to bring them here to you and your island."

Trebac continued to implore his people to hurry as he spoke, and anticipating Incres' next question he explained. "I had my scouts follow you when you left our settlement. And your little warrior told me as much as I wanted to know, that this was the island he had mentioned." Incres matched strides with the old man as they neared the lake. He had no choice but to try and get these panic-stricken people across to the island. But could he in time? And how far away were the Hunters? Inwardly Incres cursed Trebac for drawing the Hunters here. If he could not get them across in time they would be trapped.

Wolf rushed to meet him. "Do you want me to climb back up the hill, Incres, and see if the Hunters, for I believe it to be no other, are in sight?"

"Quick as you can, Wolf, and if they are, we must put up a fight here so that all may have time to cross over."

Wolf looked quickly around in all directions. "But where are we to halt them, Incres, the ground is open all the way to the lakeside?"

Incres smiled at his young friend. "Now we'll see if your boast as an archer is as empty as your head."

Pretending to be offended, Wolf pulled a face, this was the Incres he knew of old.

"Take what men of the tribe are left here, and together with those of the Louma who carry bows, position yourself some way up the hill. Protect us with your arrows until I can get all the others across, but do not leave it too late and have yourself cut off from the rafts."

The first of the returning rafts were now over half way across. Incres turned to the old man. "It will take a long time for all your people to cross from here, Trebac, leave me your best warriors to help keep back the Hunters when they arrive while I have one of my men guide your people to the other end of the island, where there are more rafts. I fear it is their only hope of crossing before your pursuers get here, if as you say they are not so very far behind."

Incres called out to Arno who was closest, "Lead some of these people to our other landing place and have them cross as quickly as you can. I hope to do the same with these people here."

"Take the most able with you, my friend," Trebac suggested. "Leave the less able here with me. Should the Hunters arrive before we are safely across, then so be it. It is better to die here free men rather than slaves to the accursed Hunters."

When Arno had gone, Incres turned his attention to Wolf on the hill, awaiting any sign from him that their enemy was in sight. When there was none, he shifted his look to the lake where the leading raft had almost reached the shore. "Hurry your people to the raft, Trebac," he urged the man.

"Incres!" And by the way Wolf was pointing, Incres realised that the Hunters were now in sight.

Incres quickly formed his men into a defensive line to protect those scrambling on to the raft, some of the older ones slipping back into the water and having to be hauled aboard.

"Your men fight only with spear and shield, old man," Incres complained in some disappointment, as their new allies stood in line beside his own warriors. "The Hunters have bows and will not come within throwing distance of your spears. It will be up to us to keep them at bay until all are safely on the rafts."

Trebac treated Incres's comment with disdain. "My bowmen were commanded to remain behind so that the rest of us could escape. If the Hunters are now in sight, then my men have done their duty…. with their lives."

Blanching at the justified rebuke, Incres turned his attention to the hill. "Wolf and those others up there have height advantage; that should help keep the Hunters from coming too close."

Incres scanned those who were still to cross, at children crying at the knee of their mothers and old folk huddled on the ground staring forlornly into the distance. An arrow thudded in to the ground, well short of where he stood but enough to tell him that their opponents meant to attack.

"Let them come within range of Wolf on the hill," he called to the line of men, unslinging his own bow from his shoulder, and wishing he had his Asan sword and shield.

Steadily the Hunters came on, three score or more, well outnumbering Incres' and Trebac's force. A hail of arrows blocked out the sun as they rose and then dropped towards them, forcing Trebac's warriors to put up their shields to protect themselves, but there was no need, as all fell short.

Now it was Wolf's turn. Using the advantage of the hill, his little band let loose their arrows, felling a half score in the front line of the advancing Hunters, a second volley hitting home again before they had time to turn and run out of range.   A cheer rose from the Maru ranks.

"That should hold them for a time." Trebac had a smile on his face. "Perhaps we shall have a chance to get everyone across."

Incres was not so optimistic. "It will be difficult when it's our turn to board the rafts; we'll be at the mercy of their arrows. Wolf, I hope will remain on the hill as long as he can." He gave a nod in the direction of the hill. "Those up there will have to make their way to the foot of the island and get themselves across from there."

In the distance a horn sounded, evidently signalling the imminent arrival of the main band of Hunters.

"Here they come!" Trebac said fearfully, his earlier optimism having quickly evaporated. "We cannot hope to hold back such numbers."

As if taking courage from the heralded arrival of their reinforcements, the enemy archers in front of Incres and his men drew stealthily forward, to be met once again by a hail of arrows from the hillside, except this time the Hunters, instead of turning and running, came on at a rush, their spearmen holding their weapons at the ready. Trebac's men hurled their own spears, bringing down some of the attackers, but in turn suffering some dead and wounded warriors. "Hold, men, hold!" their old leader shouted at them, moving to the front of the line, just as Incres and his two tribesmen let loose their own arrows, hitting those who had drawn closest to Trebac and his men.

Again Wolf's men on the hill took a heavy toll of the advancing enemy, until at last, having had enough, they retreated to await reinforcements.

The rafts, Incres noted with a quick dart in that direction, were now on their way back. With any luck the remainder of Trebac's tribe should get safely across, but as for himself and those men at the lakeside he was not so certain. Not unexpectedly, the Hunters also saw the returning rafts, and drew closer, hoping by doing so to draw Incres and the warriors nearer to the shore-line and therefore further away from their allies on the hill.

Now that they had been reinforced by the arrival of their kinsmen, the Hunters charged forward. From the hill, Wolf and the others shot as quickly as they could, and again brought down those in the vanguard, but still they surged forward. Incres and his bowmen added to the tally of the dead, but all the while found themselves being forced back towards the landing place.

The rafts had no sooner neared the shore, before Trebac's tribeswomen were wading out to meet them, babies held close to their chests, as they struggled to reach safety. Others, including the old, waited resignedly, praying that the crafts would draw closer. Arrows twanged into the wooden deck beams; one hit a woman in the back, and as she screamed in agony she tried to thrust her child to another, but the woman ignored her and pushed for the safety of the raft. More arrows hit the stationary rafts, as the Hunters came relentlessly on. Happily one raft was already heading back to the island, while the oarsmen of a second helped haul the terrified women aboard.

Incres knew at once that it would be hopeless for them even to try and reach the rafts under such heavy fire, and even so, there would be no room. Withdrawing to the rear of his line he signalled to Wolf to escape, as he did not want him and his band to be surrounded by numbers of Hunters detaching themselves from the main body to attack the hill. Another glance at the rafts told him that almost all those who were not warriors were boarding the last raft. Now it was their turn to get away, as they couldn't hope to hold off so many warriors.

Incres found Trebac at the front of his men awaiting another Hunter onslaught. "We must leave now, old man. Most of your people are now safely on the rafts. We must take to our heels and run round to the foot of the island, where there are more of our rafts, but we must hurry or our position will be no better than it is here." As he spoke, he let loose a final arrow at the advancing foe.

As one at Incres' command, all turned and followed him as he ran. A wild cheer at their backs let them know that the Hunters had taken up the chase. Fast though he ran, he occasionally stopped for a few seconds   to shoot into the midst of the chasers, or to help someone who was wounded. By his side Marc let loose an arrow before taking off again.

"I have only two arrows left, Incres!" the man gasped out.

"I am no better off, friend. How we are to hold them once we reached the rafts I don't know. We need to put more distance between us and them." It was as if Wolf had heard him, for just then a flight of arrows struck the chasing Hunters. "Wolf!" Incres cried, "He's shooting from amongst the trees!" For indeed a volley of arrows had come from amongst the trees that ran a short distance from the shore. This gave Incres and his men a much-needed breathing space, as Wolf and his surviving companions darted in and out between the trees, effectively slowing down their pursuers.

At last Incres and the warriors had almost reached the landing place where three rafts were beached ready. A warrior helped Trebac along, the old man clearly exhausted by the long run to the foot of the island.

"We are almost there, old man, do not give up on me now." Unable to speak, Trebac waved a weak hand at him, and struggled on.

Still the Hunters came on, and again Wolf and his bowmen kept them at bay, but it was now time for them too to reach the lakeside before they were cut off.

"Now is the time to use those last two arrows, Marc," Incres shouted to the man by his side. "One, Incres," Marc replied, his eyes on the cautiously approaching Hunters. "One is all that I have left."

"Then make it count, friend, when Wolf and the others run from the trees across that open ground to join us here."

"I have three arrows left, Incres." One of the other tribesmen handed Marc an arrow. "Tell us when to fire."

Incres backed slowly towards the loaded rafts, hearing urgent calls at his back to hurry.

It was then that the Hunters chose to attack, and as they did so Wolf and his four remaining tribesmen dashed across the open ground to where Incres stood waiting by the last raft. Both tribesmen and Incres fired into the advancing mass at the same time, even so, Incres was not certain that Wolf and his men would reach the rafts before the advancing Hunters cut them off.

Arrows were landing all around Incres and his band as they rapidly loosed off their remaining arrows to protect Wolf and his men as they ran towards them. Suddenly one was down, and Wolf slowed to help him to his feet until another arrow found its mark and he had to let him go.

Incres yelled to his friend to hurry, fearful that he might have to stand helplessly by to watch him die. Splashing into the water, Incres caught hold of the timber deck of the raft, where willing hands pulled him on board.

Another splash, and there was Wolf, thrashing about in the water. A man on the raft thrust out his spear to him and gratefully Wolf grasped it and held on.

"Incres!" Wolf cried, gulping in water as the raft dragged him into mid stream, "you know I can't swim!"

"Now is the time to learn, friend Wolf," Incres shot back at him, scarcely able to believe that this extrovert was being serious for once, and despite the situation could not suppress a laugh at the worried expression on the struggling man's face.

Arrows thudded into the woodwork, hitting one man who was late in holding up his shield. Slowly, almost too slowly for the huddled men, the raft drew out of danger, Incres, reaching down to take hold of Wolf's arm as he grimly held on to the spear. At last they reached the island.

Wolf, dripping water, his face pale, waded to the shore.

"I am glad to see you safe, Wolf," Incres grinned at his friend. "And I vouch I have never seen you so clean before."

Wolf glared at his leader. "Words fail me, my friend!" And he turned away with Incres's laughter ringing in his ears.

"Incres! Wolf!" Myna and Woona came running to meet them.

"You're both safe!" Woona cried, burying herself in Incres's chest, while Myna gave her man a hurried kiss on the cheek.

Serious once more, Incres strode towards the bustle of the settlement, winding his way through wounded, old people, weeping women and children; coming at last to where old Trebac lay, his white flowing hair matted with blood.

Incres knelt down beside him. "You are hurt, old man?" he asked softly, his words scarcely audible above the incessant noise, as he touched the once snow white hair.

"It is not my blood, friend Incres," Trebac quietly assured him. "My hurt cannot be seen so easily."

Incres did not know what to say, except to express his profound concerned for the old man. "I must see to our defences. I shall seek your advice when you have rested awhile," he said softly

Then, once more the warrior leader, he turned to Arno. "Have all the warriors assemble close to the landing place, and as quickly as possible. "His voice was now loud and authoritative as he spoke, and as the man moved swiftly away, called after him: "And, Arno, have that great swimmer of lakes come to me here."

Arno gave a chuckle, for he had seen the fearless bowman's floundering effort to remain afloat.

A little later, arms akimbo, Incres ran an eye over the assembled warriors. "Thanks to our unexpected allies we now number just under three score. Not many against such numbers as the Hunters over there." He jerked a thumb in their direction. " However, they still have to get here, and land, that is when they will be easy targets for our bowmen."

"What about the other landing place where we first met and fought?" a man of Trebac's tribe asked.

"We have a watchtower there, friend, and we shall know whenever they leave the shore over there. Though it's here that I fear they will strike, and when they do we must be ready."

"How long do you think it will take them to build enough rafts, Incres?" one of his own asked.

"Two days, maybe three. You men of the tribe of Trebac see to your own. My people will help feed and shelter you, though I fear many may have to spend the night under the stars. We will have fires lit, and this and the heat of the day should keep you reasonably warm."

As they moved away, Incres turned to his own tribe. "Wolf, now that you are dry," and he heard the laughter of all the others, "take charge of what bowmen you have. See to it that we have as many arrows as possible. If you think we are short, have more made. You don't have much time, friend Wolf, but all hinges on your bowmen halting the Hunters before they can get ashore.

Arno and Marc, see to the hunting of game, " he went on. "We have too many to feed from the limited stores which we have. Also, see to it than none feed their bellies too much."

When the warriors had set off on their various duties, Tomolon came to him. "You believe we have two or three days, Incres?"

"It will make no difference, Tomolon, we will be ready. And should they beat us on the shore we still have that." Incres nodded proudly at the fortified settlement. "I believe it might come as a shock to our friends the

Hunters. What say you, friend Tomolon?"

Tomolon studied the building. "Then we shall find out if our workmanship is good enough, my friend Incres."

Three days had passed and still there was no sign of the Hunters attacking.

"Perhaps they mean to starve us," Tomolon suggested as the two men stared across the still waters of the lake.

"They don't know exactly what we have here, Tomolon, and there is no way that they will, until they attempt to cross, when we shall welcome their curiosity in a most unfriendly way. No, Tomolon, they wait, but why I do not know. As yet I have not heard or seen the crash of trees to tell me that they mean to build rafts."

"Perhaps they will leave us be, Incres, and move on to easier kills," Tomolon suggested with a hopeful sigh.

"I doubt you believe that, Tomolon my friend, for you are not a fool."

Once you said differently to me," Tomolon reminded Incres with a wry smile.

It was the sound of the horn across the water early next morning that brought the curious islanders to the water's edge, Incres amongst them. "It would seem that Arcana has arrived,"Wolf murmured, at the sight of the long line of warriors descending the hill to where his Hunters were camped, each column preceded by warriors carrying long poles with the Hunters' symbol of the boar's head mounted on the point. Incres nodded agreement as Woona's grasp on his arm tightened. "They are so many, Incres," the girl gasped.

Trebac of the Louma came to stand beside them. "Now we know why there was no felling of trees," he stated simply.

"They awaited the honoured one." Wolf gave a sarcastic laugh pleased by the name he had just thought of.

Arcana, for it could be no other, gently rode his mount to the water's, edge, where he and the rest of his horsemen fanned out in a long single line.

"He can study us all he wishes, Incres," Wolf mocked, "but his horsemen will be as useful to him as a man's tit."

Incres joined in the laughter of those around him. It was good to see so many smiles, he thought, for only the Gods knew what tribulations were in store for them.

"How long do we have Incres?" Tomolon asked, his eyes fixed on the other side of the lake. "Three…maybe four days." He gave a shrug. "We must keep them at bay until the corn is ripe, for if we come under siege we will need all the food we can gather or hunt for." Incres turned his back on the lake. "Once we've eaten, we'll meet for a council."

The early darkness of the autumn evening had fallen by the time the warriors met. Incres stood facing the semi-circle of men squatting by the fire.

"Now that Arcana himself is here we can expect an early attack," he began. "Wolf, you must take Marc and a few others to hunt in the woods. Now is the time to store the game that you will catch....and it must be plenty."

"Now you can show off that skill with the bow that you are always on about." Marc smiled wickedly across the flickering camp fire at his fellow tribesman.

Before Wolf had time to find a suitable answer, Incres had resumed. "We must also put the women to the task of fetching water from the lake. I'll put Woona in charge of this task. We'll need all the jars and skins we have to hold water."

"We should dig a ditch inside the settlement, Incres, and fill it with water" Matu suggested, "which we could use to put out fires should it come to that."

"This I can do," a tribesman of the Braskan volunteered.

Incres nodded his consent. "You'll need some men to do this, you cannot hope to do it alone."

"We must have men to keep watch, Incres," Trebac cautioned. "We cannot take for granted that we have three days or more."

"I agree with friend Trebac," Tomolon said in support.

"Yan," Incres addressed the youngster who sat with his friends at the fringe of the fire, "you and your friends will take the ponies to the watch-tower and carry any messages back to us that may be necessary."

"Leave it to us, Incres!" In the firelight the boy's face shone with pride at having been given such an important task.

"Two of you will be enough at one time- three, if you think so,

Yan," Incres encouraged the boy, who shifted excitedly at this additional responsibility, only to receive a mischievous nudge from his friends.

Incres poked at the fire with his toe. "So now that we have arranged guards, hunting for food and the storing of water, is there anything other that must be attended to?"

Wolf swallowed: Incres the leader asking his warriors for their opinions? Was the man mellowing? Or was he now not altogether sure of himself?

These questions were answered early the next morning, as Wolf left for the day's hunting. "Wolf, be as quick as you can, we need you back here to help dig a trench around our settlement. "Incres' voice had an edge to it as he stared across the lake to where another tree had crashed to the ground.

Wolf raised an eyebrow. "It will take until the winter frosts to dig a trench that long, Incres."

Incres swung sharply on his friend. "Not that long, or we'll all have perished by that time. Wolf felt a sinking in the pit of his belly. "You think we won't be able to stop them from invading our island, Incres?

"You've seen how many they are; do you think we can ever hope to halt them? Savage them, yes..."

"But if we could hurt Arcana…wound him sufficiently… make him think again….perhaps?"

"Perhaps…perhaps.." .Incres jeered at his friend impatiently;.
        "Our safety depended upon our island remaining secret." The young leader made a gesture of resignation with his hands. Disconsolately, Wolf turned away, for if Incres thought they were doomed, then there was no hope.

This is what he had been waiting for, weather such as this. Blown by a cold autumn wind, rain slanted down upon the waiting men. Incres gave the silent command and the men shoved off in the two rafts from just under the watchtower. One headed for the black outcrop of rock that stood like a jagged tooth just under a bow-shot away from the opposite shore, the other carrying himself and seven others towards the Hunters who were camped there.

Incres prayed that the moon would keep hiding behind the clouds for all hinged on them making the shore unseen. He wiped the stinging rain from his face and peered into the night.

Marc pointed with the short axe that they all carried. "There," he said simply.

The curtain of rain parted briefly and Incres saw the enemy rafts tied together by the shore. Hurriedly he scanned the bushes behind the craft for any enemy guards, seeing none he increased his stroke, quietly urging on the others.

They were soon close to the shore, and Incres leaped into the freezing cold water closely followed by the others. Swiftly, the lines holding the enemy craft were cut, tied to their own rafts, and pushed out into the lake.

In less time than he had allowed for, Incres and his crew were paddling furiously away, but not before a cry of alarm went up and the shore was engulfed with fighting men.

Incres knew they were not far enough from the shore to avoid the arrows that must surely follow their discovery. Already warriors were rushing into the water, to throw their spears in their direction. Incres dug his paddle deeper straining with every ounce of strength he had, the weight of their captured raft in tow appearing to slowing them down almost to a halt.

"Incres!" Marc shouted a warning, and Incres and his men knelt to hold up their shields against the storm of arrows cutting through the night sky. Then they bent again to their paddling. "Wolf," Incres whispered, and as if his friend had heard his silent prayer through all of that maelstrom of rain and shouting, he saw some of the enemy on the shore go down as Wolf and his warriors fired from the safety of an outcrop of rock.

A warning cry rose from those on the mainland, where some were already running along the shoreline to get behind the rock outcrop where Wolf and his party sheltered, but not before a second volley had brought more of them to their knees.

"It's time to be gone, Wolf," a breathless archer urged. "They will soon be behind us and their arrows will reach us from the shore."

Ignoring the advice, Wolf loosed off another arrow. "Let us make the best of it while we can, Rua, we may not be given this chance again."

Rua bit his lip, one anxious eye on the shore as he fitted another arrow to his bow.   In contrast Wolf was enjoying himself, as one after another of the dreaded Hunters fell before his skill. Then, at last he too knew it was time to be away, as men scattered back into the safety of the trees.

With a last look towards the dark turbulent waters of the lake, satisfied that Incres and his men were out of range, Wolf scrambled down to where their own raft bumped against the rock. And in no time they too were heading back to the safety of their island.

"Pull the rafts well inshore," Incres called out to his men as they leapt ashore. "We mustn't lose them to the swell."

The willing hands of those who had waited apprehensively for the return of their fellow tribesmen pushed at the captured craft, all straining and heaving until they gained the tree line. "Wolf!" Yan cried in delight, "you are not hurt!"

"And why should I be, little scout?" Wolf replied with a laugh as he helped haul his craft onto the pebbly beach.

"I thought you had fallen asleep, friend Wolf," Incres teased, as he hauled on a line beside his friend.

"I thought to let you know friend Incres, how little you can do without me." The men around the two roared with laughter, not as much at the jest but in sheer relief at their good fortune. "They won't be so cock-sure of themselves now," Wolf declared, straightening his back, now that his craft too was securely beached.

"You took their rafts from them…and killed how many, Wolf?" an eager Yan asked, his face beaming with pride at his hero.

"Do not ask him, Yan" Incres cut in, laughing, "or he will most likely tell you it was at least half of Arcana's army."

Again there was laughter from all around. Then, just as abruptly, Incres turned to the boy. "If you are on watch, young Yan, make sure that what we did this night does not happen to us." With this sobering thought Incres left the boy as he strode off in search of Woona and something to fill his empty belly. Although tonight's venture had been a success and had lifted the spirits of the men, he feared it was nothing more than a small dent in Arcana's armour.

"Ten days, Incres, and we can reap the corn," Tomolon told his leader.

They were walking by the island's rocky shore some way north of their settlement, the purpose of which was to assure the young leader that there was no landing-places other than the two where they already kept watch for the Hunters.

"One could land here if desperate enough." Tomolon's statement did little to comfort Incres, and immediately the man regretted having further worried his leader. After all, did he not have enough on his mind.? "Though I believe they would pay dearly for the attempt," he hurriedly pointed out.

"Even if they pretend to land, Tomolon my friend, it would be enough to draw some of our warriors away from the more obvious landing places. This we can't afford to do, as we'll be hard pressed enough to halt the Hunters as it is." He threw a rock into the water. "Ten days you say, before the corn can be cut? Then, we must do our best to survive long enough to see that this is so."

Sweat dripped from Incres' naked torso as he scrambled out of the ditch where he and the rest of his men had toiled since early morning. Taking a sip of water from a deerskin, he sauntered into the settlement.

Woona stumbled in her haste to meet him. "Incres !..Incres!" the girl called out, clearly concerned about something.

"What troubles you, woman?" Incres asked harshly. His back ached and he feared the ditch would not be completed in time.

"It's Lia, woman to Nedin," Woona began nervously.

Incres did not hesitate in his stride as he spoke. "Yes, woman, I know them both. Are they not of the Brascan?"

Woona nodded in agreement. She hurried to walk beside him.

"She has not long since had a child….a boy."

"And so?" the impatience in the man's voice further frightened the already nervous girl. "She would ask…no, it was her man who should ask you…"

"Ask me what, Woona?" For a moment he halted to stare down at the girl. "Quickly now, for I must inspect the hole that we dig to hold water for emergencies." Before the girl could answer, having already dismissed the matter as trivial, Incres suddenly asked her, "How many jars and skins have you and the women prepared to hold water when we are besieged?"

Woona was unprepared for the change of subject, though alarmed that Incres had spoken of being besieged as if it had already been ordained by the gods.   "You think it will come to this, Incres? "she asked, her voice shaking.

Incres walked on. "You haven't answered my question woman!"

"What question, Incres?" Woona furrowed her brows.

Incres lost his temper. "The question I have newly asked," he flared up.

"I will find out for you, Incres."

Woona watched the man she had known all of her days stride away, although now she thought that she had not known him at all…at least not now.

Chapter 4

Arcana scowled at the man kneeling at his feet. "The islanders took the rafts from under your very nose!" The man said nothing, the only indication that he had heard was to tremble even more. "Who is he that leads on yonder island? Do you know of him?"

"Yes, Lord, he is of the Maru, his name is Incres," the kneeling man said hurriedly, anxious to please.

"The Maru? My understanding was that they were under the protection of the Asan and were cave dwellers there? Is that not so?"

The chastened man took courage to raise his head, albeit slightly. "This is true as you say Lord, though I believe some led by this Incres left to settle on yonder island, as I am told that he has no love for the Lord Meruk for what he did to one of his own."

Arcana gave a brief nod, then gestured that the man should rise. "It was done in revenge for what this Maru had done to his son, I seem to remember?"

"Yes, Lord," the man said, struggling to his feet.

"You have been very careless, Ramseen. Now I must attack the island from one side only, for if I have to await the rebuilding of your rafts, this Incres would see that as an act of weakness. "Here the leader of the Hunters pointed an angry finger at the offender. "You will lead that attack, Ramseen, and don't bother to return should you fail."

The Hunters attacked at first light. Eight rafts swept across the still waters of the lake on the island, archers ran to conceal themselves amongst the bushes and behind trees close to the shore.

"I have not witnessed anything like this before, Incres," Trebac confessed his uneasiness to his leader.

Sweeping his gaze along the shore-line then out to the

approaching rafts, Incres asked in a voice verging on anger that his thoughts should be so interrupted at this vital time. "What have you not witnessed before, old man?"

"Women with bows! Do you believe they can hit anything at all?"

"They have been well trained, my friend." Incres's voice still held a hint of anger as he answered.

"And if they can, will they do so with warriors such as the Hunters charging at them? I think not, Incres. A woman's tasks are to cook and mend and care for her warriors' children, not this." Trebac threw out a hand to where the women crouched behind some bushes a little way to his left.

"Then we'll soon find out," Incres breathed.

Spread out in a line the three enemy rafts carrying the bowmen halted just offshore, with the remaining craft a little way behind. At a signal from Ramseen the bowmen released their arrows at their unseen foe, in the hope that they in turn would reveal themselves when they returned fire.

When none was forthcoming, Ramseen signalled that they should row closer. Again all was silent upon the shore, and the leader ordered that they should fire again. This time it brought a cry from one of the women who had been hit. Another screamed, and Trebac shot Incres a look, inferring that he knew that this would happen. This was no place for women, only warriors

Another flight of arrows filled the air, and Incres saw one of his warriors fall, hit by an arrow in the chest. The rafts were speeding closer now, firing as they came, the spearmen's rafts following close behind.

"Now!" Incres cried, and with Wolf at their head all the archers loosed off their arrows, toppling some of the Hunters into the water. Still they came on, led as before by the bowmen, the spearmen's rafts now ploughing their way across the still waters until they were abreast of their fellow tribesmen, all now anxious to be ashore. Again the islanders fired their deadly arrows, this time hitting spearmen as well as bowmen.

Now from high up in the trees the islanders' archers fired their arrows down on the unprotected heads of those on the rafts. However, the Hunters had also found targets, as some who had become over-anxious ran out from the cover of the trees.

"Back! Back!" Wolf shouted , enraged at this folly, and ordered another volley

"We cannot hold them, Incres!" Tomolon exclaimed.

Incres took a hasty look at the rows of spearmen a little way behind him, all anxiously awaiting his command to attack the Hunters as they leaped ashore. He knew the man was right, there could be no stopping these men, they were too many.

However, it was Wolf who came to the rescue. Running to the end of his line of bowmen, he pointed at a raft now side-on to where he stood, shouting to his archers to fire at those steering the craft. Then, finding Yan unexpectedly at his side, ordered the boy to run to the other flank and tell the bowmen there to do likewise.

In no time at all the craft closest to where Wolf stood lost direction and thudded into one of the others as his archers took their toll of the rowers. Everywhere men were catapulted overboard or died from the storm of arrows from the shore. Another volley hit an oncoming raft filled with spearmen, who struggled to keep their balance, as yet another vessel rammed into their side.

The warrior Ramseen saw what he believed to have been a certain victory suddenly turn into turmoil as one after another of the rafts collided. Men in the water struggled to stay alive as Wolf's archers continued to fire their deadly missiles. Here and there a floating body bobbed to the surface, an arrow protruding from front or back. That he was a dead man was all that Ranseen could think to mutter to himself, Arcana would have his head, of this there was no doubt.

"Back! Back!, fools!" he shouted, spittle foaming from his mouth. Clumsily the rafts swung around as the surviving oarsmen struggled to get their vessel out of arrow-range. The spearmen, whose craft had been a little way behind and who still had their oarsmen, had already turned around and were rapidly making back of the mainland. Ranseen watched them speed away. It was the last he was to see of them as an arrow took him in the throat.

"You've done it! You've done it Wolf!" Yan cried, dancing excitedly in front of his hero, amid the cheering from those around.

"Well done, friend Wolf." Incres added his praise. "I'll never doubt your brain-power again!"

"Brains as well as brawn?" Wolf teased, smiling at the compliment.

Incres turned at Tomolon's appearance. "How many have we lost, Tomolon?"

"Four of your own, Incres, and the one you heard scream was his woman. She too is dead. Also there are a few wounded"

Incres knew the couple to whom Tomolon referred, and for a moment saw them again as they took a final farewell of each other before running to where they must stand and fight.

"The women fought well." Though his voice had been quiet, Trebac had heard him.

"Then tell them, Incres. Tell them all how well they have fought this day."

For some reason Incres felt aggrieved at the other man. Perhaps he was still in shock from the day's battle. Or was it because he had not thought to do so himself?

"They did not fight for me, Trebac, they fought to save themselves. They must remember how it was done when the Hunters return…as they will."

Wolf was still glorying in their victory as he came upon Incres helping to dig the ditches that he was certain would be vital to their survival.

"We won't need this, Incres my friend, the Hunters will never reach this far." He grinned broadly as he pointed to the ditch.

Annoyed that others had heard this latest absurdity, Incres paused in his work to glare at his friend. "You think not, hero Wolf?" he mocked the man. "We beat them off last time because all our warriors were here while none were at the other end of the island. Next time, when Arcana has replaced the rafts which we stole from him, they will attack both places at once. What then? Halt them with half our force? I think not."

It was out before he had time to think about what he had said, and he cursed himself for being a fool. Jude would not have quashed their spirits as he had done. He saw the look on the faces of those closest, all which seemed to say 'what was the point in digging a ditch if their leader believed they were already doomed.'

Incres quickly rushed to make amends. "Except if you can persuade Yan and his friends to build a few more of those giant 'slings' as he calls them." He gave a laugh, hoping to dispel the dampening effect of his previous remark.

"I will do my best. I know Yan will be more than happy to do so, instead of digging a ditch that will not be needed." This time it was Wolf's turn to mock as he went about finding his young protégé.

Woona stood beside her man on the shore. They had come to rest a little from their work, through in truth there was no rest for her warrior leader.

"They will come again, won't they Incres?" she asked quietly, her head on Incres's shoulder.

"This they no doubt must do, Woona; Arcana cannot let it be known that the lowly Maru and their friends have stood up to him. No, he must see us all dead or enslaved."

The shudder that Woona gave was not for herself our even for her friends but for this man she loved. Should Arcana take Incres alive, what he would do to him did not bear thinking.

"I have much to do, Incres, I must get back." Woona turned to walk back up the path, halting as she tentatively asked a question she had asked before but had received no answer.

"Nedin has asked that his woman should not help to dig the ditch as she is still weak from her first-born."

His eyes still on the lake, Incres replied "You can find other work for this woman? "whom he knew was of the Brascan.

"I can, Incres, if you command it."

Incres turned, and to the woman's surprise he smiled at her. "Do you think that I should command it, Woona?" He gave a little shake of his head. "If only that it were not so. What would I not give that it should not be so."

The man's eyes stared beyond her, the words said as if to himself. "So many lives.

"Incres has said that Lia may do other chores," Woona told Myna as she dipped her deerskin into the lake.

So Incres has said that lazy bitch Lia does not have to help dig the ditch, Myna muttered angrily to herself. Then what about herself and all the others who had toiled each and every day since Incres had commanded it? The lazy bitch could work as hard as anyone had she a mind to. Why did Tomolon not do something about it? He had known, as she herself had, how lazy the woman had always been, almost as lazy as her quarrelsome man. Well, she would not get away with it, she would see to that, now that Woona had asked that she find her an easier chore.

Incres watched Yan drop the pebbles he had in his hand one at a time upon the same spot. That the boy should be so idle when there was so much to be done before the Hunters came again angered him. Yet, he had to admit that the boy and his friends had toiled long and hard to build more giant slings, as they were known.

"Yan, what are you up to? If you have so much time to waste you can always help finish digging the ditch."

If Yan had heard Incres he made no sign, as with head bent he went about dropping the pebbles upon the path.

"Did you hear me, boy!" Incres barked at the silent youth.

It was then that the galloping pony appeared, to be drawn up on its haunches by a boy rider."Two score. Not as good as last time," Yan retorted scornfully at the panting boy. Dismounting, Yan's friend stroked the sweating animal. "Perhaps next time, but we must rest the beast, eh?"

"Why are you two playing yourselves when there is so much that needs to be done?" Incres chastised them angrily.

As if aware of Incres for the first time, Yan swung round to his leader, a hurt expression on his face at being so accused. "We are not playing, Incres. We practice at knowing how long it will take to reach here from the watchtower at the top of our island. You said that it was up to me to see that you were well warned should the Hunters win to the shore."

"And how will dropping stones help you determine this?" Incres asked, now a little calmer and somewhat curious.

"First time it took thirty dropped stones to reach here, now our best is nineteen," Yan explained, pointing at a heap of stones on the ground.

"I suppose I should be impressed by your ingenuity. But tell me, my young learned one of the giant slings," Incres gently mocked the boy, thrusting his face close to his, "how do you know when your young friend leaves the watchtower?" He poked Yan playfully in the chest, fully expecting the boy's expression to change at this supposedly demoralising question.

"By that," Yan pointed, and Incres turned to where another youngster waved a spear at him. "They stand by the path and signal when the rider is about to leave....it might not be quite..." "Enough ...enough," Incres laughed, throwing his hands in the air as he made to leave. "I am sorry that I misjudged you."

"And my friends?" Yan called after his leader, "all of them?"

They had completed the ditch, now all they had to do was to wait for Arcana to attack. "Five days, Incres. Why does he wait?" Tomolon asked his leader.

Incres shrugged. "A hunter can take his time when he is sure of his kill."

"Perhaps he means to starve us, and if so, he has made a mistake."

"No, my friend Tomolon, Arcana cannot wait all that long, for the winter will soon be upon him and he cannot hope to feed all of his warriors."

They had not long to wait. Next morning Incres heard a warning horn sound as he roused himself from his slumber. Wolf ran to meet him as he himself headed for the gate, and his friend turned to run by his side.

"They are many more this time , Incres. I think Arcana himself is with them," Wolf gasped as he ran.

"We can only spare twenty men to defend the north landings." Incres drew breath. "Tell Yan he must have someone ready here with a pony to tell those up at the north landings when to leave if we here have to retreat to the settlement if we are beaten back." Incres swallowed, nd took another deep breath as they reached the gate. "I don't want them to be left outside when we close the gates."

"'I'll tell the boy, Incres, when I find him, which I expect will be by one of his beloved slings."

Incres managed a chuckle. "They do well Wolf, though this time I think they will have to load ten times faster if we are to hold back Arcana and his Hunters."

Incres leaned his sword and shield against the tree, then shuffled through the dead leaves to stand with the other archers in their accustomed place behind trees, now almost winter bare.   Unlike the Hunters whose numbers seemed to swell with every attack, their own continued to shrink. Incres ran his eyes over the short line of archers on either side of the path that led to the shore, then back to where Tomolon and Trebac waited out of the firing line of the archers with their spearmen.

Trebac saw him looking, and gave an encouraging wave of his spear, while the man next to him pulled his skin cap closer about his ears. Most however stood silently staring through the trees or down the path at the enemy now drawing closer to the shore.

Suddenly, and without the slightest warning the air was filled with burning arrows that showered down upon them and quickly ignited the dead foliage around their feet. Smoke too, stung their eyes, forcing Incres and his warriors coughing and spluttering back from the shelter of the trees.

So that was why Arcana had not attacked these last few days; Incres thought, he had waited until the wind blew towards the shore to blind them with smoke, and at the same time hide his own men from their arrows.

"Forward, men! We must not let them land!" Incres shouted, the words scarcely audible above his own coughing and the crackle of burning wood, as he forced himself back into the smoke.

Their hands held before their faces against the heat, Incres's archers followed, but it was to no avail, they could not see where to aim.

"Quickly, to the path!" Incres called out, already running in that direction, but the narrow path gave them little respite from the now fiercely burning trees and shrubbery, and led by Wolf, they let loose their arrows at an enemy now alarmingly close to shore.

Still they came. Now and then a rock hurled from Yan's slings would splash into the water, to land close, or in some cases into the midst of a crowded raft.

"We can halt them, Incres, if we retreat back up the path. They will have to come almost in single file with the fire raging on either side." It was Trebac who had shouted the words at him. Incres loosed off an arrow and stepped back beside his friend while he fitted another arrow to his bow. "No, Trebac, Arcana will try to outflank us." Incres fired as he spat out the words. "Leave a few men on the path, take half to either flank and halt the Hunters when they try to land by the rocks. Go now!" he shouted at the man.

Now men were leaping from the first of the rafts that had reached the shore, wading through the water to instantly disappear as if some sea monster had swallowed them up. Only here and there a body writhed in agony or a head bobbed lifelessly in the cold winter water, as the first wave of attackers fell on to spikes beneath the water.

It was as the terrified survivors turned to scramble back onto to their bobbing rafts that Wolf and his archers did their deadliest work. Previously restricted to the path, they now ran onto the beach, firing as they went.

Still on the path, Incres signalled to where Tomolon, behind him, awaited his command, who, with a wild battle-cry, rushed his spearmen forward in support of the battling Wolf.

From where he stood Trebac noted with relief that Incres had correctly judged Arcana's reaction to his men falling into the submerged spikes, for, upon his not knowing how many of these traps lay between his warriors and the path, he must try and find other landing places, which was why Incres had sent him and his spearmen to either flank to prevent their landing. Below him the first of an enemy raft had thudded into the rocks and before any of the Hunters could scramble ashore his spearmen had done their work.

Trebac signalled that the spearmen should follow him to where another raft was edging closer to the shore. Here the rocks were not so steep, and eager hands were already grasping at the nearest vegetation and rock to pull themsleves ashore.

Trebac waved to one of the few bowmen with him and the man let loose a flurry of arrows, tumbling men into the water as the remainder desperately pulled their craft away from the rocky shore before more succumbed to this bowman's deadly fire.

Soon Trebac saw with satisfaction, and more than a little relief, that the remaining rafts were pulling away and heading once more for the safety of the mainland.

"We've done it!" the old man shouted with glee. "Come, let us see what's happening at the north of our island, seeing as how we're closer to it than the others, for who knows, they might be in need of our help."

Trebac headed his warrior spearmen to the watchtower, where, long before they had seen what was happening there, they heard the loud noise of battle. Bursting into the clearing by the shore, Trebac saw in an instant that they were just in time, as the defendants there were hard pressed by the Hunters, who at last had gained a foothold on the shore. With a wild cry Trebac's warriors launched themselves at the invaders, who for a while held their ground against this unexpected reinforcement, until with another wild cry Wolf appeared at the head of his bowmen.

Not many Hunters survived this last charge, the remainder fleeing back to their raft, but not before Wolf and his archers had brought down a half score more before the swiftly retreating crafts were out of range.

Arcana could scarcely control his temper. That a few savages had dared to defy him was beyond belief. He must end it and swiftly, as with each passing day it became more difficult to feed his men, now that winter was upon them. Arcana aimed an angry blow at a passing warrior who with head bowed struggled to drag his wounded leg towards the campfire. "Cowards!" he shouted at everybody within earshot. That he, the mighty Arcana, should be so shamed further fuelled his anger. The next attack must be the last. He must conquer the island before news of this continual resistance by such a miserably low tribe as the Maru travelled further, even to the ears of the Asan. Tomorrow, he decided he would end it all, and there would be no mercy. He would slay every last man woman and child as a warning to those who would oppose the Mighty Arcana.

For as long as Incres could remember he had never really known what it was to be happy, nor had he known a place that he and his tribe could have called their own. Yes, perhaps for a little time at the caves. Incres sighed.

Had it been pride that had him forsake the caves, and not out of anger at the death of his friend Dryan? Had he in fact brought them here to their deaths? Had Jude been right when he told them that they must swallow their pride and learn to live in harmony with Meruk and the Asan?

Incres kicked at a pebble as he stood on the beach and stared across to the smoking campfires of the Hunters. A high shrill burst of laughter from a little way beyond the outline of burned trees arrested his attention. The leader walked through skeletal trees that thrust black fingers in to the sky to where Yan and his young companions were busy bending another sling in readiness for another attack. One dropped the boulder he had been carrying at the foot of the bent sapling, saying something to Yan that made the boy and those closest to him laugh. They had not seen him and he continued to watch as they happily went about their work, envious of their boundless energy.

Although he had not known any happier times than those that he spied upon, he felt a sudden empathy for their naivety, and dread for what was likely to happen to them when Arcana eventually defeated them. That his own fate was already sealed he had no doubt. But to those happy youngsters was their fate to be a life of slavery or death at the hands of the evil man who had pursued his tribe inexorably? Once again his thoughts turned to Jude. Had he remained within Meruk's protection these young folk would have had a chance to survive…well at least Yan, for he had not known the others who had come to join them on the island. Sadly, Incres carefully backed into the scant coverage of the trees.

It was as Incres reached the settlement gate that he became aware of angry voices from within, the loudest of which he recognised as that of the man Nedin. Apprehensively, Incres walked through the gate.

"You! Incres! You!" Nedin stormed, extricating himself from the group that stood in the centre of the compound. He strode angrily towards the leader, his head thrust forward, eyes blazing. "You have killed Lia my woman…. left my child motherless all because of your accursed ditch! You had her work there. Now she has bled to death!"

"It grieves me to hear of your woman, Nedin."

Taken aback by Incres' apparent contrition, Nedin drew himself up, for he had so wanted a confrontation with this man. "Are these words all you can think of, oh great warrior of the Maru?" he sneered.

If Incres was stung by the rebuke he showed no sign. Instead, he looked to where Woona stood with some of the other women one whom he believed to be holding Lia's wailing child. Woona returned his look and gave a slight shrug of her shoulders, spreading her hands as if to say she did not know what the angry man was talking about.

"Your woman was told that she did not have to dig the ditch and that other tasks would be given to her," Incres replied curtly.

"I do not believe you, Incres! No one told her, for had this been the case she would have told me." Nedin's angry words served as a challenge to Incres.

Incres drew himself to his full height: he had had enough. There were much more important things than this to occupy his mind. "Whether or not Lia told you is of no importance now that she is dead, but Nedin, your child is not. And if you think much of its life you must be ready to defend it". Incres cast a swift eye around those gathered there. "We all must. Now let us all go about our business."

He could have asked Woona there and then if she indeed had relayed his command to Lia, but if he'd found out at that time that she hadn't, it would only have exasperated the situation. Such were his thoughts as the gathering slowly dispersed, some, with a few disgruntled comments as they went.

"You have made an enemy there, Incres my friend," Wolf said drawing closer to him. "Perhaps it is not just Arcana's warriors that you should be wary of.....eh!" Wolf gave a chuckle, though Incres knew that his friend was deadly serious in his assumption.

Woona swept back the skin door covering of Wolf's shelter outside the settlement where they had chosen to live.

"Why did you not tell Lia of Incres's decision to let her have easier tasks, Myna?" Woona's words were like darts hurled into the girl's back. Myna did not turn round as she stirred the pot, only a slight stiffening of her shoulders told Woona that she had heard her. "Now Incres has made an enemy out of Nedin, as if he has not enough trouble across the lake." Woona lunged forward, spinning the kneeling girl round. "Do you hear me, Myna!" she spat out.

Tears came into Myna's eyes. "I did not wish her dead, Woona. It was…it was only..." She halted. Suddenly the tears were gone to be replaced by an anger that Woona had never seen before. "She always pretended sickness,

Woona, to avoid working like the rest of us. Tomolon did nothing when we told him. His answer was always that she was weak…had been since birth." Myna choked back her anger. "She was not weak, Woona, only lazy, that is why I did not tell her what Incres said, though I did not wish her dead."

Woona released her hold on the agitated girl. "Now Incres must make his peace with Tomolon, for Lia was of his tribe." She took a step towards the door. "You must tell both men that it was you who caused the death of Nedin's woman, even though you did not seek it.

"No! No, Woona!" Myna jumped up, her hands outstretched,

pleading. "Please do not let them know. You will shame me in front of the tribes."

Before Woona could answer there came the sound of the warning horn. "It must be left for now, or perhaps forever if the Hunters break through this time." Woona barked. "Get yourself to the settlement while you can."

For a second Myna hesitated. "But the pot?" she gestured panicking.

"Bring it with you, and if it's still hot you can throw it down on the Hunters," Woona shot back angrily. "Now let's go."

The matter of the death of Lia was temporarily forgotten by Tomolon as he stood beside Incres, a hand held against the slanting rays of a weak early winter sun. A slight breeze shook his cloak as he spoke. "Arcana will not be stupid enough to come straight for our shore, Incres, as he now knows where our traps lie. Therefore, he will make for the rocks on either side of them as he did last time."

"I think not, Tomolon my friend." Incres pointed to where Arcana's fleet of rafts headed for the head of their island. "He is going to attack our landing place in the north where he knows there are no hidden ditches. This he will have learned from those who gained the shore yesterday."

"Do you think so?" Trebac had joined the two men. "Perhaps he means to fool us into believing this, so that we will send most of our warriors to confront him there."

"Let's just wait, my friends. Let's wait and see if any of the rafts turn this way, though I doubt if they will"

Incres was soon proved right, for Arcana's entire force was headed for the north of the island.

"Yan!" Incres called to the boy as he ran past," your slings are of no use here; have you any that will fire at our other landing place?"

His chest heaving, the boy answered without hesitation "Sla and Moorco are already there. We piled our stones there when we finished here yesterday."

"Well done, Yan," Incres nodded, proud of the boy and his friends.

"Have one of your friends station himself here with a pony. Have him tell us if any of the Hunters' rafts head in this direction."

"This I will do, Incres," the boy answered enthusiastically: and to Incres, it seemed no more than a game to the youth.

Incres led his warriors to the head of the island. A fierce wind tore at their clothes and a bitter rain drenched them as they ran. In the distance came the rumbling of thunder.

Once he'd reached the defences, Incres hid his bowmen behind the shoulder high rocks that stood a little ways from the beach. Woona threw him a nervous little smile as she took her place beside the other women, her bow at the ready. Incres's heart filled with emotion as he looked at the slender figure, shivering as much from fear of the impending attack as from the chilling wind that had suddenly sprang up, to throw freezing rain at them as they waited.

He knew or guessed what his own fate might be should they lose; the women, he feared, would fare the worse. Incres gripped the metal sword tighter. If the gods decreed it, so be it, though many Hunters would not see it happen.

"The fire will not light," Marco shouted to Incres. "The rain has soaked the kindling we had ready."

"It must, Marco, if we are to play Arcana at his own game. Now give it another try"

Dismayed that this part of his plan might not work, Incres turned his attention back to the approaching rafts, now mid-way across.

Wolf came from where he had been standing beside Woona behind the rocks. "Arcana must breed his warriors overnight Incres," he chuckled.

"How many Wolf?"

"Eight score," Trabec answered for him.

"I should say the same," Tomolon agreed.

"And we have less than two score including the women and boys," Wolf clicked his teeth.

"Then you must make every arrow count, friend Wolf," Incres

answered, tight-lipped. "Do I not always, my ungrateful friend?" Wolf replied, with a mock frown.

The foremost of the Hunters rafts had now fanned out as they approached. These were only partially filled with bowmen, as other warriors kneeled in front to protect them with their shields while they shot their arrows once within range of the shore.

"Is that fire of yours ready, Marco?" Incres called out anxiously, his voice scarcely audible above the mounting wind and a rain rapidly turning to sleet.

"Just about, Incres, it burns a little," the man shouted back.

"If it doesn't, Marco my friend, I will give you a tail to wear with my spear," Wolf called out to him cheerfully.

A sudden gust of wind rocked the first of the Hunters' rafts, the slanting rain making it difficult for both sides to see one another. Incres wiped the cold stinging rain from his eyes as another gust of wind hit the oncoming crafts.

"It's no use Incres, the fire has gone out!" Marco kicked out at the smoking embers in frustration.

"It can't be helped Marco. Besides, I suspect our arrows wouldn't have burned anything at all on the rafts in this weather."

A flight of arrows suddenly whistled out of the leaden sky, landing with a thud upon the beach in an attempt to draw Wolf's archers' fire. A flash of lightning lit up the sky, reflected briefly by the lake's surface. Thunder crashed at regular intervals, the entire scene unreal to those who waited on the shore. White-foamed waves rose and fell, tossing the small crafts about. Suddenly, a raft heaved upwards under the mounting swell sending its occupants, who had been fighting to retain their balance, into the water. Other craft bumped into one another, as oarsmen fought to turn their rafts away from the shore

"Now, Wolf!" Incres cried, and Wolf, with his bowmen at his heels, broke from the cover of the rocks to the water's edge, firing arrows at the men on the rafts, whose sole purpose now was to head back to the mainland, the battle already forgotten.

Wolf was enjoying himself, loosing off his arrows as swiftly as he could and urging the others to do likewise, there being no danger for them; all Arcana's warriors had on their minds was to be away from this storm and the deadly fire of arrows.

Tomolon for his part took his spearmen down to the water's edge. Although no raft was in range of their spears; all he wanted was to see the destruction of the foe.

"Is that not Arcana I see in the water?" Marco shouted in Tomolon's ear.

"It is indeed, friend Marco, but I grieve to see that he has been hauled aboard yonder raft. Better that he had drowned and with him all our troubles, but the gods have done enough for us this day." Tomolon let out a sigh, with the thought of what could have been.

To add to their unexpected victory, a boulder from Yan's sling landed squarely on a heaving raft, catapulting the entire crew into the turbulent waters of the lake, the sight of which brought more cheering from those on shore.

Then suddenly there were no more craft to be seen. Once again, they had repulsed Arcana and his Hunters.

All the island people, except the wounded and the infirm, stood silently on the beach, their faces turned to the mainland where black palls of smoke spiralled up into a clear blue sky, all that was left of the Hunters shelters.

Smoke too, swept across the opposite shore where Arcana had set fire to his rafts.

"They are gone." Trebac spoke as if to himself.

Incres did not answer; instead, his eyes slowly travelled over all who stood there, now not so many. Away to his right, Yan chased his sister Gista, followed by other laughing children into the blackened trees, their victory already forgotten.

"He will return, of that there is no doubt," Tomolon declared dully.

"Come, oh miserable one, let us at least enjoy the moment." Wolf said cheerfully, clapping the man on the back and winking at Incres. "Shall we not feast in safety tonight?"

Incres nodded. "It has been earned- not too much eating though, for we still have a winter before us."

"You were ever the carrier of dark thoughts, my friend," Wolf teased. "How many times have you predicted that the Hunters would take our island?" He threw a hand towards the further shore. "Where are they now, my friend...eh?"

A raft on the mainland suddenly burst into flame bringing a cheer from those around. "You don't grudge them their victory, do you, Incres?" Wolf gestured towards the cheering tribes-folk.

"No, no, Wolf; However, when you are done with celebrating, we must start to defend ourselves again, for when Arcana returns, he will bring with him every man he can muster."

Despite the weather having held bright and chilly since the storm that had undoubtedly saved them, Incres would not let his eager warriors cross to the mainland, for fear that this was a trick by his enemy, who might be more confident of defeating them by meeting them on open ground.

However, an immediate situation arose which diverted their thoughts from the mainland.

"Incres! Incres" Gista called out as she ran to meet him and Woona. "Wolf says that you must come quickly to the compound," she gasped, having run her fastest to give him Wolf's message.

Darting a quick look of concern at Woona, Incres swiftly followed the running girl back through the gates of the settlement where, at its centre, Nedin held court; who upon seeing the young warrior chief stopped holding forth and turned to face him.

Nedin's eyes blazed with anger, as if daring Incres to command him to stop. When he did not, Incres gestured that he should continue. "It is as I was saying," Nedin started defiantly, his eyes still on Incres, "that we must be gone before Arcana returns, and this time the gods will not protect us." A murmur of agreement greeted Nedin's words, encouraging him to shout more pithy comments at the gathering. "If we remain here we will surely die. Think not of yourselves, my warriors, but of your women. Do you wish to see them raped? That is, if you are spared torture, or submit to being slaves of the Hunters until death overtakes you."

As Nedin halted for breath from his tirade, Trebac met Incres eyes through the crowd , waiting for him to halt the man before he had gone too far and had persuaded this gathering to quit the island. Still Incres remained silent.

Unnerved by Incres's silence, though he now had the ear of the gathering, Nedin drew to a withering halt. "So I for one am for quitting this death-rap, and the sooner the better, for I mean to be well away from here before

Arcana in all his might and wrath returns." Again he cast an eye of defiance at Incres. "And no one…." his voice rose. " and I do mean no one will stop me."

"You would be so ungrateful, Nedin, to one who has saved your life?"

Tomolon's voice was harsh as he pushed his way through the small crowd.

For a moment Nedin looked puzzled until his chief went on. "Have you forgotten such a small matter, Nedin, of the Brascan, in so little a time?"

"No…no" the man stammered. "Of course I am grateful, as all of the Brascan are who were saved by the Maru from the snow. I…but we cannot be slaves to them. Have we not shown our gratitude by standing by their side against the

Hunters? And to you, Incres, whom we chose to follow from the lands of the Asan, but we don't want to die here!"

"You fought well, Nedin, as bravely as any man here." Incres came a little forward to address the man. "So it is your right should you so desire to leave. I'm sure no one here will prevent you, not even Tomolon, your own chief."

Puzzled by the lack of opposition from the man he so much wanted to humiliate, a man whom he believed to be the reason for the death of his woman, Nedin fell silent.

"However," Incres went on quietly. "I would counsel that it would better that you and those who would also choose to leave should wait until the weather warms. Why leave now, with no where to rest or shelter? At least here you have both." At this logic there was a murmur of approval.

Nedin was at a loss for words, for what Incres had said made sense. Even so, he could not appear to lose face. "So be it, Incres." He pointed a finger of warning at his adversary, "but only until the earth warms and we can be on our way." And there it was left.

It was a day when the sun had gone to sleep. The winter, though harsh, had not been as severe as it had been in the past. Nothing remained of the enemy camp now, all shelter and rafts having been destroyed at the command of the leader, the islanders having taken anything that was left of the once great camp that they deemed to be of value.

Incres kicked at a patch of black ash poking through the last of the melting snow. "Let's climb up yonder to the trees, Wolf, though I doubt all prey will have gone to ground. We'd better not venture over far."

Wolf grinned at his friend. "Ever the cautious one, eh, Incres? Arcana will still be away toasting his toes at his own fireside and will not return until the weather warms." He grinned again and turned away.

It was as they were making their way through the trees further up the hill that the figures came suddenly upon them. Instinctively Wolf unslung his bow, as did all around him. However, the approaching strangers- for there must have been close on a score, showed no sign of alarm, but continued to stride forward. The foremost, a tall man, had a broad smile on his face.

"You are of the Maru?" he asked cheerfully, as if having found a treasure.

"You are right to think so, friend," Incres returned, his curiosity aroused by this man's pleasant demeanour.

"Would it be too much to believe that we have reached the home of the great Incres?" The man pointed towards the island in the distance, the broad smile still on his face.

"The great Incres!" Wolf'boomed beside him.

"Yes he is, to us and all in the North; that is why we are here to join the man who has the courage to face Arcana and his Hunters."

Incres studied the man. Should he be suspicious of this happy-go-lucky character?

"We have journeyed from the far north, where even there they have heard of this Incres. We have left our women behind so that we will not be overburdened, and more able to fight. So, tell me friend, when can I meet this great man?

"You already have!" Wolf laughed and the others joined in.

The strange leader's face took on a startled look. "You are Incres?" he asked, pointing at him.

Incres admitted that he was. "It would help to know what you are called, if you mean to fight by our side," Incres asked not unkindly.

"I am Debu. We have no tribe, only a gathering of folk as poor as ourselves."

"Why do want to fight with us, Debu? Arcana, I believe has not yet reached as far north to where you live. Surely it would have been wiser to remain there...until...until all is over here?" It was Wolf who had asked the questions.

"This, we could have done, but if you were beaten here, it would only be a matter of time before Arcana reaches our homes. But, together if we are to halt him.... bleed him some, then perhaps it will be enough."

Incres saw the reasoning and nodded. "Very well, you may join us. However, there is not enough space on our island for you all; therefore, I suggest that you make camp a little way down this hill. You will see the island well enough from there, and if danger threatens you will receive ample warning of Arcana's coming. Also, you may visit our island, for there is still work to be done on our defences. This, and the fact you must learn to train with us when you come to help defend our island."

"It's a good idea, Incres, my friend. This we will do."

That night Trebac walked with Incres along the shore. "You are not quite sure of this Debu, Incres?" he asked, gazing across the still waters of the lake in the direction of the man's camp, where pin-points of light flickered across the water from their camp-fires.

"I suppose it could be a trap, Trebac. If these men are in the employ of Arcana, it would be to his advantage to have them amongst us here on the island."

A cold wind ruffled the steel grey waters of the lake, as Trebac replied. "I think it wise what you have done. But how to be sure? We can't afford to be mistaken, and have to watch our backs if the fighting starts."

"I'm well aware of that, Trebac my friend... I'm well aware of that."

However, it was to Yan's friend that Incres was to be grateful for the answer. Yan appeared at Incres' door in the settlement, where Woona stirred a pot set over the fire.

"Yan: this is a surprise! Is Gista not with you?"

The boy shook his head. He had no time to speak of foolish things with a woman, not even Woona whom he loved as a sister, not when he had great news to tell Incres - news that would make Wolf proud of him.

"It was Incres I came to speak with." Yan's voice had taken on a tone of importance as he lifted his head.

"Then you shall, young man. "Incres came down the ladder from where he had been dozing in their loft. When the weather became kinder, he intended to move back out to his old shelter where there was more privacy. He reached the foot of the ladder and leaned against it.   "And these words you would have with me?"

"These men who have come to help us beat Arcana...those that live on the hill..."

"You have seen them?" Incres asked, raising an eyebrow.

Yan nodded his head vigorously. "I spoke with the one called Debu. I like him," Yan gave a broad grin. "He is funny." Incres gestured impatiently for the boy to go on. He was hungry. "My friend Opu, tells me that his father had told him that Hunters …true Hunters, bear a strange design upon their arm. This they are given at birth." He gave a gasp as Incres threw his hands in the air

"Of course!" Incres exclaimed. "Have we not seen these same marks upon those Hunters we have slain? Though I had not realised that this was to tell which warrior was indeed a true Hunter. But tell me, Yan," Incres, his hunger forgotten, stepped towards the boy, placing a hand upon his shoulder. "This friend of yours, does he know if those who are taken and forced to fight for the Hunters also bear these same strange markings?"

Yan shook his head. "No. But I do." The boy gave a mischievous grin, relishing the importance of what he was about to say.

Woona gave him a playful nudge. "Out with it Yan, before Incres here loses his good humour," she urged the boy, giving her man a sly wink. Incres pretended to be angry. "Do as the woman says, Yan, I am hungry, and when I have not eaten I am not someone you should annoy."

Yan took a precarious step back. He had only wished to impress his leader. "It is only…it is…." Incres wriggled his fingers in a gesture that he should hurry. Yan swallowed. "It was the day…" Now he wished he had not remembered. "It was the day that we found the stranger." He had not wished to say that it had been the day that Incres had slain Dorcus.

Incres saw the boy's discomfiture. "I remember the day, Yan. What about this stranger?"

"He had a burn mark on his arm…he said all those who had been captured and forced to fight for the Hunters had them seared upon their skin. It was the mark of a spear. Do you not remember?"

Incres clicked his fingers. "Of course, Yan, I do remember". He squeezed the boy's shoulder in appreciation. "Well done. It's what I needed to know." With this the happy boy left his leader to his meal.

"They do well." Trebac caught Incres unawares as the latter stood on the shore, gazing across the lake in the direction of the Asan.

What was Lyra doing right now, Incres wondered? Had she

already been bedded to the chief of the rival tribe in order to keep the peace between them? Incres shuddered at the thought of someone else coupling with that beautiful body, especially if it was someone whom she did not love.

Incres spun round. "I didn't hear you approach, Trebac, my thoughts were elsewhere." "You're still unsure of our new friends over there?"

Incres made a gesture, letting the other believe that is where his thoughts had lain.

Trebac drew closer to his leader. "Why not let some cross, and let them see what we have here? We need every warrior to help build the defences you mentioned at the last meeting." Incres turned his back to the lake. "You think this is wise, Trebac?"

"Let only a few come at first, Debu amongst them, as he acts as leader there. "Besides," The man chuckled, as they began to walk back to the settlement, "they have been without women for some time."

"If you think it wise, Trebac my friend. As you say, we need all the warriors we can get. It is that I do not trust them that worries me, but their weapons. Most carry slings and short spears and bows. Their shields will not stop Arcana's arrows. Others carry only stone axes."

"You must call a council, Incres, when you have thought out the best plan to defend our island."

"This I will do, my friend." Incres put his hand on the man's shoulder. "Has Nedin said anything about his leaving, now that the earth grows warmer?"

Trebac gave a shrug. "I do not know I had hoped that Tomolon's idea of putting him in charge of our winter stores may have helped to change his mind, though I fear it may have only fuelled his pride."

"I hope not, Trebac, for if he and those of a similar mind choose to leave, it could give rise to our new friends on the hill thinking again. I should not like to answer their questions; to explain how this came about, and why some of our number see only their death in awaiting Arcana's coming."

"Then let us hope the man has changed his mind. Perhaps he has already done so, now that there are others who have come to fight Arcana."

"I am truly in the hands of the gods!" Debu threw his hands in the air, his eyes gleaming at the sight of the settlement. "Even if Arcana were to invade your island, Incres my friend, he will get no further!" Debu laughed loudly, encouraging his fellow tribesmen to join in.

"Let's hope that is so, Debu. Now let me show you what must be done."

Over the next few weeks more warriors came to join Incres, which meant having Yan and his young friends go about these strangers in a way that grown men could not, in order to see whether any bore the marking of the Hunters.

None did.

Eight days later the first of Incres' scouts returned with the alarming news that the mighty Arcana was on the march, this time with an army that could be counted in their hundreds. In order not to spread panic, especially with Nedin about, Incres swore his scout to secrecy.

"The first of the scouts believes Arcana will be here in five or six days time," Incres informed Wolf. He drew in a deep breath. "His army greatly outnumbers our own, Wolf" "Perhaps so, but we have many more here to greet him warmly," Wolf, ever the optimist, assured him.

Incres shook his head. "Though we number close on nine score, with a few more joining us each day, it will not be enough, not with Arcana knowing where we have put stakes under the water at our landing places. So, he will probe for other places to land. We cannot hope to defend them all. All of this we will speak of at tonight's council.

Chapter 5

Incres's eyes swept the warriors sitting in a half circle around the camp fire. "Arcana is now only four sunrises distant." He halted to let the low murmur die down as they digested his words. "Debu, you will move your warriors here to the island. Remember that Arcana knows where our hidden stakes are under the water from his previous visit." He halted again, this time to let the ripple of laughter die down: "He will seek out other landing places. Fortunately we have already dug ditches and placed our stakes where we believe these places to be.

Debu, you will set up your camp close to the places that I wish you to defend." The man nodded.

Incres swung round "Yan, I wish you to choose someone else to be in charge of the slings." At the boy's crestfallen look, he went on, "for I have a more important task for you. As there are three landing-places besides those of the original two, we will not be able to defend them all in great numbers, so, Yan, it is your task to carry the messages from those who command at the landing places who need more aid, to Trebac, who will position himself close to the centre of the island, where he will wait with what reserves we have. You will of course need more helpers, and as we do not have enough ponies, choose those who are swift of foot. This I will leave to you." To further swell the boy's pride, the leader went on: "Include our new friends in this, even if they're older than yourself."

At first Yan could not believe what he was hearing. His eyes darted from his friends to meet those of Wolf. What would his hero make of this? He was scarcely aware of Incres continuing. "Debu, have your warriors hunt and bring what game they catch on the mainland to Nedin here. He will be in charge of all stores. Hunt well, for what you bring must last us until winter. Or until Arcana decides that he has had enough." Again there was laughter, this time much louder.

"We need more arrows made, Incres," Trebac pointed out.

"And spears," another quickly followed.

"Then get on with it!" Incres spoke quite sharply. "You don't need me to issue an order for something so obvious. This also applies to those of our new friends who fight with slings." Now aware of how his previous words had sounded, Incres softened his tone by adding, "I think they will not lack for stones," he smiled. "Are there any more questions?"

Trebac made his way through the dispersing warriors to Incres. "So, you believe me too old to fight, Incres, that you have put me in charge of our reserves?" Trebac sounded offended. "No, no, Trebac my friend, but I need a steady head when it comes to the number of warriors that you must send to the most dangerous areas. I, myself will be at the northern landing place, for I know not how Debu and his warriors can fight, not with such weapons as they have."

"And should they mean to betray us, you will have placed yourself in the most dangerous position." Trebac's voice was little more than a whisper, as he now understood the implications of the younger man's decision to put himself and not someone else in such danger, if Debu and his warriors were to betray them.

The rafts were piled to overflowing with wood for their camp-fires, skins and brush for shelters, and such animals as they had caught, all these for the oncoming siege

"We have more than enough to last us from now throughout the winter, Incres." Woona aired her thoughts, as she stood beside Incres on the shore.

Incres surveyed the hustle and bustle of the warriors, the women carrying the water jars to their fortress,-the high excited cries of the children. "No, we still do not have enough. Nedin!" Incres walked to where the man was directing those warriors carrying the carcasses of deer, wolf and hare, all the while tallying the count. "How say you, Nedin, do we have enough to keep us throughout the summer and to the other side of winter?" Incres awaited the man's reaction to his implication that his Stores Master intended to remain on the island.

His eyes still on the carriers Nedin gave a nod. "If we live to see it," he said curtly.

Incres had to bite his tongue in case he should blurt out that Nedin and whoever had a mind to were still free to leave, but the truth was he needed every warrior that he could muster. It was best that there should not be any sign of dissent, especially to those who had travelled far to fight by their side.

Nedin's glare towards Incres never left his face. Did this man think him a fool, that by putting him in charge of the stores that this was the reason why he had decided not to leave? In truth it now made more sense to stay than leave, others having reasoned that Arcana would find them wherever they might be. Besides, he still had his motherless child to think about. Therefore, if only a few decided to leave with him it would be seen as a victory for Incres, and a further humiliation for himself. "There will be enough. We will not need so much when there are not so many of us left."

Incres contained his anger as he spoke. "You believe Arcana will defeat us, Nedin…take our island, after all the work we have done to build this?" The warrior leader threw out a hand in the direction of the settlement.

"That will not halt him. Nothing will. Arcana cannot be seen to be beaten by the likes of the lowly Maru, it would see the end of his power: this he cannot allow." With this final taunt the man swung away.

It was in fact eight days before the first of Arcana's army arrived. Hidden from the enemy's sight Incres's new allies watched the Hunters start about the business of erecting their camp, in the exact spot as they had done previously.

Wolf gave Incres a nudge. "Now for some fun," he laughed, those around him joining in. Wolf's anticipation of the fun to come was quickly justified as the first of Arcana's warriors fell into the traps dug by the islanders who had anticipated where they would build their shelters. At once all was mayhem as more warriors fell onto the spikes in the traps, so that all work came instantly to a halt, no one knowing which way to step.

"That should slow them up a bit," Tomolon guffawed. "I swear we have caught close on a score. It's a pity, Arcana was not amongst them."

Arcana, when he arrived next day, was beside himself with rage. Not only had he lost warriors to the traps by the lakeside, but also to those who had gone in search of trees to fell for the rafts. Once again, Incres had out-smarted him.

"This Incres will pray to die when I have him here," Arcana bellowed, kicking out at a rug at his feet in the large shelter that had been built for him, some distance away from the shore. "How many have we lost, Baracas, to these ..these," he stammered, spittle running from his mouth.

The tall warrior quaked before his master's wrath. "Close on two score I believe, my lord" "You believe!…you believe!" Arcana mimicked the quivering man. "Two score? It is fortunate that I can have them easily replaced."

He flung out a hand in the direction of the island. "This time his pitiful little tribe will not stand against the might of Arcana, not when I am wise to his little tricks."

Baracas dropped his eyes to the earthern floor, afraid that this tyrant of a master would see in them the thought that he had not been wise to the traps Incres had laid for him here on the mainland.

"Tomorrow," Arcana was saying, "we will put an end to this Incres and his kind."

Sixteen rafts swept the coastline of the tiny island, each searching for a suitable new landing place.

Arcana noted the stone walls and sharpened stakes at three of the points, dismissing any notion of landing there. His silent anger rose at this man Incres, who had dared to defy him, and he thought again of what he would do to him when he was in his power.

The attack on the northern landing place came first, and Incres was relieved when Debu and his warriors withstood the hail of arrows from the rafts, waiting until the Hunters plunged ashore before cutting down the foremost of the attackers with their slings, and those who had not fallen into the newly dug underwater pits.

However, it was at the opposite end of the island that Arcana's main force struck. Here the shore-line, though dotted with huge rocks, afforded a place to land, and by sheer weight of numbers the

Hunters gained a foothold upon the island. Now these same rocks that had earlier been an obstruction now became a place of shelter as Arcana's Hunters fired their arrows from behind these granite shields.

Tomolon, recognising that they would soon be overwhelmed, sent the first of the young messengers back to Trebac, who in turn, after dispatching a score of warriors to Tomolon, had Yan inform Incres at the head of the island.

Now that Incres had seen the calibre of the men that Debu led, he was not apprehensive of leaving him, while Yan rode with him to the foot of the island so that he could see for himself what was happening there.

"Although our bowmen have kept their heads down, and have prevented further rafts from coming ashore, it will not be long before the Hunters strike again," Tomolon explained to the young leader from behind the shelter of one of the scant trees that grew there. "We only just succeeded in repelling their last attack, due to the timely arrival of our reserves."

Incres took in the scene at a glance. "We have two score at most." For a moment his gaze lingered on the dead lying by the shore, not all of whom were Hunters.

"Our new friends fight well, Incres, but they lack the weapons of the Hunters...and their numbers."

Even as he spoke a line of warriors sprang from behind the rocks to hurl themselves at the defenders. A few were caught in the open by the island bowmen, but not before some in their turn were pierced by arrows from the

offshore rafts. Incres cut down the first to reach the trees, and swing sharply on another, his sword hacking at a third, while a fourth endeavoured to get behind him, only to be pierced by Tomolon's spear.

"They are more coming ashore, Incres." Tomolon gasped for breath as he lunged at another Hunter. "We cannot hope to halt them again."

It was at this moment that a hail of arrows struck down this new wave of invaders. For a moment Incres was taken aback by this unexpected help, until he heard the familiar laughter of Wolf.

"Must I do all the work on this island, friend Incres?" Wolf shouted at him from behind a clump of bushes a little way up the slight slope to the shore.

Incres turned to give his rescuer a hasty wave before fending off a fresh opponent, who now realising that he and a rapidly diminishing number of his companions were now almost completely cut off, turned to run back to the shore, only to be cut down by Wolf and his bowmen. It was all over for a time.

"Your plan appears to be succeeding my lord," Baracas said, anxious to please his master. It was now seven days since Arcana's last attack on the island. Now he contented himself by pretending to launch his rafts at various landing places, both by day and at night; reasoning that the defenders would be too tired to repel his main attack when it came. He'd give it another few days, then, he'd mount his greatest attack so far. And this time there would be no retreat.

"We cannot hope to keep this up, Incres," Tomolon was telling the young leader. "Arcana is playing with us. Four mock attacks last night, and three today. The men are near to exhaustion, constantly rallying to the sound of the horn. They cannot take much more."

"It needn't be necessarily so, Tomolon," Trebac offered. "We already have warriors camped near to the landing places. Why not have them bed down closer to the shore? This way only when the rafts are within bowshot need the sentinel sound his horn. Otherwise, let the men sleep."

"Your plan is good Trebac," Incres said, nodding his approval.

"Then why not play Arcana at his own game?" Trebac suggested with a mischievous grin. "Do not light any camp-fires at all at night. Have him think we're dead or are asleep with exhaustion."

Incres laughed. "Another excellent idea, Trebac. We could have our cooking done by daylight, when the smoke is not so readily seen amongst the trees. Let Arcana tire himself out." The men voiced their agreement. Now for a good nights sleep.

"The island is dead." Arcana strode to the water's edge, Baracas by his side. "Their warriors no longer rush to the shore when we draw near, nor do they sound their horns. Is it a game they play with us, Baracas?" he asked angrily of his warrior.

"Perhaps, my lord."

"And I see no camp-fires at night. How can this be, man?"

Unsure exactly how to answer his unpredictable master, Baracas stared across the breadth of the lake. " It may be that they are all victims of a plague, my lord. Perhaps the gods have smote them down."

Arcana swung round angrily. "Do you expect me to believe such rubbish, man? That it is the work of the gods? If they all happen to be dead, it is by my hand and not by the actions of the gods, and this I will prove to you when we attack tomorrow. The time for playing games is at an end."

This time it was for real, all of Arcana's rafts were heading for the island, his entire army poised to attack.

"Yan, have everyone gather at the foot of the island!" Incres shouted to the boy, as he and the warriors roused themselves at the sound of the warning horns. "Find Trebac, tell him all the women who can fire a bow must also be there, and any woman who thinks herself strong or brave enough to hurl a spear. Wolf will also know what to do"

"You want no one at the other places, Incres?" the boy shouted back above the rush of people.

"Only a single guard, for we will need all our strength to repel them this time, Yan, including your friends who are not needed for sending messages. I mean only to leave those on the watchtower at the north of our island, for

I have seen one of Arcana's rafts go there. Tell Trebac when you find him to send a half score men should he believe that they intend to land there as well. If you have need of me you will find me at the foot of the island. Now go!"

Incres was running full pelt as he snapped out his orders to the boy.

This could be their last day, he thought, as he watched Yan speed off to do his bidding.

Tomolon had already set out his spearmen when Incres arrived at the tail of the island. "Arcana means to end it here, Incres my friend." The man pointed to the rafts now within bowshot of Wolf's archers.

Incres swept a hasty glance along the line of warriors, most sheltered by the odd tree that grew there, or behind the black rocks closer to the shore. The first flight of arrows from the rafts thudded close to where they stood, to be answered by Wolf's archers downwards from the grassy banking some distance to his right. He heard a sound, and quickly turned to see that the women had arrived, and was surprised to see that Woona and Myna were amongst them, and not with Wolf and his archers. Evidently they had elected to fight beside little Gista and her young friends. That it had come to this, or more to the point, that he had brought them to this. What would Jude have done?· Then again Jude would not have brought them here in the first place-to their deaths.

He strode quickly towards them. "You women bide here, see that no one gets behind our warriors. Use your spears as best you can." His eyes travelled to the youngsters, many like Gista not more than children. What chance had they against such warriors as the Hunters? Perhaps, he should have let them remain in the settlement where they were safe, at least for the time being.   The first of Arcana's warriors were now leaping ashore, and his own warriors led by Debu rushed to meet them, while Tomolon held back his own line of spearmen. Now more of Incres' warriors were arriving from the north end of the island, but the young warrior stopped them from rushing to join the fray. "Wait until I give the order," he barked at them, his eyes riveted on the battle raging by the shore. Unhurriedly he drew his sword from its sheath, his shield held close to his body.

Matu came to stand beside him. "I believe Arcana has paid us a compliment by bringing all of his grand army to view our island," Matu chuckled, his eyes on the shore line.

"I'm sure you're right, Matu, though I fear we will not allow him the pleasure of seeing more than there is to see here," and he heard the man laugh drily.

Debu and his men were now hard pressed to hold their part of the shoreline, while others some distance to their left, were being pushed back by the sheer weight of numbers. Incres looked at Tomolon, who gave a nod of understanding and together they led their men forward in a rush, Incres to where Debu fought, and Tomolon to the opposite end of the sandy shoreline. All the while Wolf's bowmen, now aided by the women, were taking their toll from the high banking.

Incres attacked his first opponent with all his pent-up anger, killing the man with a few deft strokes of his sword, quickly turning to fend off another who had endeavoured to get behind him. Still Arcana's men were coming ashore in what seemed to the young leader, unceasing numbers. Should he order a retreat back to the settlement while there was still time? It would mean a long siege, and they would lose their crops. Angrily he lashed out at another opponent. No, they would hold them here, although it would take another miracle from the gods.

The miracle that Incres sought came from an unexpected quarter. Arcana, his raft some distance off shore, suddenly turned in the direction of his own camp, although this was obscured by the lay of the land to the young warrior.

Incres' brain briefly registered that Wolf and his archers were no longer upon the grassy banking. He heard a woman scream from behind, but could not turn as other enemy warriors came at him. Lashing out with his sword, he backed away, anxious to know what was happening behind him as other screams filled the air.

At last he was given a respite as Arcana's warriors found easier targets to attack. Swinging round he found the source of his concern. Hunters were now stabbing and cutting at the women, who, obeying his orders, were doing their utmost to prevent their enemies from getting behind him and his men. One woman screamed as a sword caught her in the belly; another, clearly hysterical, dropped her weapon and ran for her life into the trees. All the while backing into the trees, Gista, Woona and Myna stood thrusting with their spears. Incres rushed at those attacking the three women, at the same time as

Wolf and his bowmen appeared out of the woods, and together they pushed back their attackers.

"You women!" Incres called out to the sobbing shaking women, "get yourselves back to the settlement. We may have to retreat there, so be ready."

"You think so, Incres?" Wolf asked startled by his friend's comment.

"Perhaps not, Wolf, but we must be ready to do so if necessary. Besides, the women and children have done enough. We cannot ask for more."

"Perhaps we should just stay put for now?" Wolf gave an incredulous laugh, amazed by what he was witnessing, for now most of the Hunters were heading back to the rafts at the sound of a horn.

Incres knitted his brows in puzzlement as he watched them go, chased by his own warriors taking their final revenge on those too slow or too weak to make it to the safety of the rafts. Now all that remained were the dead and the dying.

"Incres! Incres!" Yan jumped from his pony before it had time to draw up. "Arcana's camp is on fire," the boy gulped, and Wolf caught him by the arm to steady him in his excitement. "Men are landing at our beach…it is they who have put the torch to the camp. I don't know who they are, Incres!" Yan stammered.

"Trebac says you must come at once!"

"Calm yourself, young Yan." Wolf shook his head while digesting what the young messenger had said. Whoever these strangers are they had undoubtedly saved the day.

Once back at the settlement, Incres found Trebac, surrounded by curious women greeting their rescuers warmly. At the sight of his leader, Trebac pushed through the babbling women.   "This is Miroco, leader of those who have burned our good lord Acrcana's camp," he beamed at Incres, gesturing to a small wiry man who came to stand before him.

"So, it's you who we must thank for this days work, Miroco, my friend," Incres smiled broadly, giving the man a slight bow.

"So you are the great Incres?" The man's eyes lit up as he gripped the young leader's forearm in way of greeting. Incres heard his friend Wolf laugh to hear his friend being so addressed.

"I am Incres, but as to great?" He gave a shrug.

"Miroco!" All turned at the shout. Debu pushed his way through those gathered there. "What brings you to Incres island? I would have thought that there would have been easier pickings for you and your robbers back up north."

This was said with such venom from one so placid that everyone was taken aback, some muttering that this was no way to greet their rescuers.

"You know this man?" Trebac asked, anticipating some trouble between them.

"It is my wish that I did not," Debu, retorted angrily.

"Incres, you must be desperate to defend your island when you rely upon such as these!" Miroco burst out angrily, taking a step back and drawing his sword.

"Enough!" Incres barked, his eyes blazing at each in turn. "Have you both come here to quarrel, or help fight Arcana?" At the rebuke the newcomer lowered his weapon, his eyes still on his foe, and Debu, who had been in the act of drawing his own weapon, pushed his sword back into its sheath.

"What is between us can wait. You need fear no trouble from me, friend Incres."

"Nor I," Miroco echoed. His eyes swept his surrounding, coming to rest upon the settlement. "You built that, friend Incres?"

"With a little help from others," Wolf laughed, intending to ease the tension.

"Will there be trouble, between Debu and the man Miroco, Incres?" Woona asked, turning her head slightly to ask the young leader, as they walked by the edge of the tree

Incres breathed in the cool night air. The heat of the summer day was leaving. His eyes came to rest by the shore where the trees, still black from the burning of the previous year, had sprouted new leaves which would soon fall as the days grew cooler.

The man Miroco worried him. Though he had undoubtedly saved them from Arcana's last attack by burning his camp, he had not liked the look he had seen on the warrior's face when realising how few they were in numbers.

Woona tugged at his arm. "I wish I knew, Woona; as if I didn't have enough to worry about. How are matters in the settlement?" he asked, changing the subject.

Woona gave a deep sigh. "Some of the women- and some of the men too," she corrected herself, complain about the lack of space now that there are so many wounded. I am happy that I live outside with you, Incres. I dont think I could stand all that noise, and not only from the babes."

"You may have to, Woona, should we have to retreat there

"Do you think it'll come to that, Incres?" The concern in the woman's voice was so intense that the warrior put an arm around her.

"I just don't know where all Arcana's men are coming from. He also has so many supplies that I fear that he will remain here during the winter. If we have to retreat to the settlement before the corn is harvested we will surely starve if he does decides not to leave."

Incres gave the woman a reassuring squeeze. "However, we must wait and see what the rascal does, now that he no longer has a camp- at least not for a while."

However, Incres was wrong in thinking that his rival would delay further attacks until his new camp was built. Anxious to defeat this stubborn enemy before the coming of Autumn, next day Arcana launched another attack at the same place.

This time, aided by their new friends, the islanders beat off numerous landings, until as night fell the tyrant warrior was forced to call off any further attacks.

"How many did we lose today?" Incres asked a weary Tomolon.

"Two score, either dead or wounded." The man leaned against a tree, staring across the water. "We must retreat to the settlement,

Incres, for we cannot hope to fight off such numbers." Incres studied the ground at his feet. "The corn is not yet ripe. We do not have sufficient meat to last from now throughout the winter. Besides, who is to say that if Arcana lands a force on the island that he will not overwinter here, or at least leave enough men to ensure that we bide within our walls."

"This is a decision you alone must make, Incres my friend, and I'm afraid I don't envy you it."

Incres wearily hoisted his shield upon his shoulder, and once again wondered what Jude would have done.

The wounded warrior dragged himself past his chief, who, full of rage, lashed out at the unfortunate man, all his pent-up anger behind the blow of his axe, cleaving the wretch's head in two.

"That....that...!" Arcana flung the blooded axe at the prone figure. "That Incres has mauled half my army. Where do all his men come from?" For the previous night the Hunter chief had witnessed the numerous camp fires burning on the island.

Baracas steeled himself for a further angry onslaught from his master, his fear heightened by the fact he had not answered. As Arcana's eyes continued to bore into him as he awaited an answer; with a dry throat, he ventured:

"He is strengthened by those from the cold north, my lord." He took a hasty step back as Arcana made to come at him. "But it may be all for the best, my lord." The unexpected statement halted Arcana. Baracas hurried on. "It will make our- your task the easier, when you can defeat them here instead of having to hunt them in their own forests and hills."

Arcana was silent for a moment as he digested the terrified man's words. This could be so. Already he had been informed that Meruk of the Asan had moved his warriors closer to his own rearguard. This of course could be to prevent his Hunters from raiding or hunting in Asan land. However he could not take the chance of being attacked by Meruk and this being so would have to leave men there to watch the man which in turn would leave him fewer warriors to attack this accursed Incres.

He thought again of what Baracas had said previously about forming a truce with Meruk, which would eliminate the threat of an attack from that quarter. Or even form an alliance, such as wedding Meruk's daughter, whom he understood to be an extremely beautiful creature. The thought brought a smile to his face. That could well be a good course to take. But what of the present?

"You, Baracas, will journey home. You will muster every man who can lift a spear. You will leave no one behind, and have them here within twenty suns. Do you understand?"

Baracas studied his feet, contemplating whether or not to risk further anger from this insane man by suggesting what was in his mind.

Relishing the man's fear but not his silence, Arcana hissed: "Do you understand, Baracas?" The other spread his hands in a pleading gesture. "Is it your intention that I leave no one behind? Not even those who would harvest the crops, my lord?"

"Let the women do so, as they have done before. Why ask this, fool?"

Still trembling, Baracas cleared his throat and spoke out. "It is just that many of the women have warriors here, who are not of our tribe, so with no one to guard them they may seek to make their escape; and when their men learn that there is no one to prevent their leaving, these same warriors may take the opportunity to desert." Baracas swallowed hard, fighting for the courage to add, "Perhaps worse, my lord, they might seek to join the accursed Incres."

For a moment Arcana could not believe what he was hearing; what this underling was saying. Yet it made sense, for it was only the threat of what he would do to their women that held these same warriors here. True, they fought well, but this was only to preserve their own lives, and not out of any loyalty to him or the Hunters. Finally he said: "Leave sufficient men behind to see that no women escape, nor any of those who furnish me with our much-needed supplies." Arcana pointed to the island. "This farce has gone on long enough."

Yan drew his sister aside. "You mustn't over-tire yourself, Gista."

The girl looked up from where she had put the clean cloth upon the fevered brow of a wounded man. "But there are so many of them, Yan, some in terrible pain." She walked to where a man lay tied to a bench, his teeth clenched on a piece of wood to help ease his agony. Yan winced at the sight of the affected leg, while a girl swatted flies away as she knelt beside the tortured man. Yan saw a whole day's pain in each flicker of the warrior's eyelids. He must have endured this - for how many days? The eyes were asking him to end it all. The boy looked away unable to endure the man's suffering. He heard a sound behind him in the open courtyard and swung round, grateful for the distraction. Incres, with Trebac at his side, halted now and again to offer a word of comfort as they drew nearer to where he stood.

"What can we do for them Incres?" Yan, spread his hands out in desperation.

"Nothing, I fear Yan. It is the price of war."

"You are wrong!" A voice shrilled at them. Startled, Incres stared at the girl rising from the wounded man's bedside. "There is a flower in the hills where we lived. Its leaves have many healing powers, and the seeds help dull the pain. You will know of this flower, Lord Trebac."   A gasp came from the old man's lips. "I had forgotten, Shana. You're right, this flower would end much suffering. Yet, how to come by it?"

"You know where to find this flower?" Incres asked, drawing closer to the girl."

The girl nodded as she took the hand of the wounded man.

"Can you swim?" Incres asked.

"That I can-and well."

"Then so be it. You will take Yan with you." Then, at the youngster's gasp of surprise, added, "For he also can swim well."

They waited until the moon slid behind a cloud. Then, and only then, did two warriors push the log a little way from the shore.

Incres laid his hand on Yan's shoulder. "It is best that you let the log drift as far as possible, then all being well you and Shana can swim the rest of the way to the opposite shore. You have the bags to hold the flowers?"

The girl unlsung the bag she had carried across her shoulder and hooked it around a small branch on the log, Yan doing likewise. "Take care when you reach the shore, more so when you journey inland as you may come across parties hunting for food," Incres told them softly.

"Yes, Incres." Yan took the girl by the hand and she gave a little shiver as he led her into the cold dark water. The warriors let the log go, and the youngsters let it carry them out into the lake, Incres watching until it was swallowed up into the night.

"Are you alright?" Yan whispered, his head resting lightly on the log.

"I'm as strong as you, boy," the girl retorted angrily, spitting water from her mouth.

Why had Incres insisted he take this slip of a girl Yan wondered, guiding their floating shield towards the shore. Of course it was because she knew the whereabouts of this mysterious blue flower, but surely there must others much stronger who could have accompanied him?

He saw the girl take a firmer hold of the log. "We can rest a spell, if you like?" he suggested, and in the pale moonlight saw her shake her head. Angrily, he swam harder. He would teach her to say she was as strong as he.

The current was not taking them closer to the opposite shore. It would be easier, he decided without the log, though it would have helped to hide them from any watchful eyes

"We'll take the sacks and head for the banking over there. This log is no use to us now." Reluctantly the girl let her grasp slacken on the short branch she had been clinging to.

"It is not so far now. You can make it."

Yan's sympathy was not appreciated. With a few deft strokes Shana kicked away from behind her protection, leaving the boy to follow.

It was further than the swimmers had thought, both having to rest a few times before they eventually began to tread water. Yan pointed to some bushes by the lakeside that would offer them some cover should their approach have been seen, and they ran towards them. Shivering, they crouched down, listening for any sound that might tell them that they had been discovered. "I think it's safe to move. We should get away from the shore as quickly as we can,"

Yan suggested, cautiously rising. Her teeth chattering, his companion agreed.

It was then the moon slid out from behind a cloud, momentarily lighting up their path. The two broke into a run, happy to feel warmth returning to their bodies. Eventually Yan drew to a halt.

"I believe this is far enough for tonight. It's too dark to venture further, and in any case we don't want to stumble upon any Hunters, after having come this far. Let's shelter here amongst these bushes"

Silently Shana slid to the ground and rested her head against the slight banking. Yan dropped by her side, as she gave a little shudder. He drew closer, intending to put his arm around her and give her the heat of his body.

Angrily, she drew away, and he rolled his eyes heavenwards, cursing Incres once again for having burdened him with such as this child. So, let her freeze. Perhaps by morning she would have realised her mistake.

They were both awake long before the coming of dawn, and happy to be on their way from the chill of the night. Yan doubted whether either had slept at all, as they plodded up and over the first of the hills. He halted and pointed to his right where the lake lay cold and grey in the early morning light, the green and brown of the trees with the island at its centre.

"I believe this is the way we should journey. Do you remember how long it took from your home to our island, when you were chased by the Hunters?"

"Three, perhaps four days. Many times we hid. Then the Hunters found us and our warrior bowmen held then off so that we could escape." Yan took her hand and she did not object. "My mother died on that last day. She was too weak to go on."

"I'm really sorry, Shana. I did not know."

The girl tugged at his hand. "We must hurry. We can't take four days, not when my father is in so much pain."

"Your father?" Horror -struck, Yan turned to look at her as they hurried on. "The one you came to stand beside when first you saw me?" Yan shuddered, as he thought again of the man with the gaping wound in his leg, and how, to help bear the pain, he had bitten down on the wood in his mouth. How long could he endure that suffering? How long had last night been to him? "We will get there long before four days, Shana, but we must also be careful."

The travellers did not halt until well into midday.

"We must rest, Shana." Yan threw himself down on the grass, and as the girl reluctantly dropped to her knees, he extracted some berries from the pouch he wore around his neck. "Here, this is all we have except for some meat Wolf wrapped in some skin for us." He held up the little sack he was carrying. "We shall have some of this tonight," he promised her.

Later that day, as the sun set behind the distant mountains, Yan cut a strip of meat with his dagger, his only weapon, and held it out to the girl. "Here. Eat. You have journeyed well today. Now we must rest."

Reluctantly Shana took the proffered meat. "We can travel further, it is not yet dark." Chewing on his own ration, Yan shook his head. "We must not over-tire ourselves. We must be fresh to journey even further tomorrow."

"You mean not overtire me!" Shana said bitterly

"Eat, woman. I am much too tired to argue."

Smiling to herself, the girl bit into her meat, amused at the slyness of the boy.

"Those are the hills of home, Yan!" the girl cried excitedly.

Yan shaded his eyes against the weak sun. "We shall reach them tomorrow, and find your flowers." He slid to the ground and opened the sack of meat.

"We can travel further today, Yan, the sun has not yet set."

Yan shook his head. "This is a good place to rest. We'll be well hidden should any of the Hunters have come this far.

"You are lazy, Yan, you know very well that no Hunters will be away up here in these hills.!" The girl stamped her feet in anger. "Have you no pity for my father and his like?" she flung at him.

Yan felt the colour rise in his cheeks. No one had ever accused him of not having done well at any task set him. "Go on if you like, but I will not wait for you on the way home when you fall asleep. And this being so, it will be you who have added more days to your father's suffering."

Beaten, Shana slowly dropped on to the dry, brown autumn grass, and without speaking, Yan held out the strip of meat to her.

It was almost midday before they reached Shana's hills of home.

"Up there,!" she cried running up a steep banking. "My mother brought me here when I was little!" She turned quickly to look down at the boy. "Hurry, Yan, we can have our sacks filled and be on our way back to the island before night-fall."

"Steady, Shana, you must have a care not to fall, for if you do I'm not going to carry you all the way back. In reply, Shana made a face and disappeared behind the crest. Shaking his head in despair, Yan followed, and there some distance away found the girl already picking the blue flowers that dotted this side of the hill.

"We should have brought more sacks; we may well need them if the fighting lasts until winter. Also the flowers here will have withered by then." The girl plucked eagerly at the flowers as she spoke.

As Yan dropped the gathered flowers into his sack he noticed the girl's slim figure for the first time, and felt a surge of desire to couple with this fiery creature. As if aware of the boy looking at her, Shana looked up, and took a sudden step back as if afraid of what she saw in his eyes. Embarrassed, Yan stooped to his flower-gathering, and Shana, a little fearful of her companion, moved away to continue her work.

Later, their gathering done, it was the suggestion that they take a look at Shana's old home before they started back that eased the tension between them. Torn between the curiosity of seeing her home again and her haste to be back to her father, Shana agreed to the former, but only from a hill-top. She didn't want to venture further and waste precious time. She guided Yan over the gentler slopes until at last they were looking down upon the settlement.

Except it was to find not only was the place not burned down but also alive with men.

Yan let out a gasp and drew Shana quickly down amongst the bracken. "Those are Hunters down there! This is why Arcana has not returned home; why he didn't let up on his attacks after Miroco burned his camp! He has all the supplies he needs here to keep him through the winter. He just has to keep sending home for more and they bring it to here." Yan's eyes gleamed with admiration as well as fear for his own folk. "Now indeed we must hurry back, if for no other reason that to warn Incres."

They ran, stumbled and ran again, all caution thrown to the wind in their haste to get back to the island, only sleeping a little at night, and at the first glimmer of light setting off on their way once more. At last, starving, for their meagre supplies had long since gone, they reached the lake.

"We must be careful not to be caught, not after having travelled this far," Yan cautioned the eager girl. "We must wait until it is dark." The boy searched the shore from his hiding place. "I see no log that will hide us and help us reach the other side."

Shana sat back amongst the tall reeds. "We cannot lose the flowers Yan."

It was the boy's chance to encourage her. He put his arm around her and she did not resist. He squeezed tighter. "I shall go to the north of the island. Perhaps I can swim across from there. Others will come and find you. Keep hidden. You must not be caught by the Hunters."

Shana cocked her head to the side a little and gave Yan a wicked smile. "You would worry about me, Yan?"

"No," he teased, in return, "I just don't want to lose the flowers."

The girl gave a soft laugh. "Be gone, boy, and do not be caught yourself." She gave him a gentle push.

Yan climbed away from the shore of the lake. Then, when high enough up the undulating slopes, lay down to await nightfall, but not before he had located the camp of the Hunters at the head of the island. Yan rolled over on to his back. It would still be a long swim, though not as long as the point where he had left the girl. He felt heat surge through him at the thought of Shana, no longer seeing her as a mere child, but someone knowing as many sunrises as himself. Eventually it was dark enough for him to leave. Quietly he made his way down towards the shore, aware of the waves of ribald laughter from the enemy camp not so very far away. There were bound to be guards close to the water's edge, fearful of an attack as there had been in the past when Incres and Wolf had burned their rafts.

Yan drew up, and sank to the ground behind a bush, as the shadow of a guard strolled slowly passed. His hearting beating fast, Yan waited until the man was well out of the way before, in a crouch, he gained the shore and waded into the cold dark water of the lake.

Yan set off, and when barely half way across realised how tired he was from the long trail that day. Turning on to his back he allowed himself to float a little, but quickly turned again as the current drove him away from the island. Again he made a few strokes, gulping water as he started to sink. Suddenly an arrow spun at him through the air, then another and another. He ducked down, his head scarcely above water, and as another arrow dropped inches away saw the direction from which it came.

"It is me, Yan!" he called out as loud as he could. Still arrows came in his direction. All this way to be killed by your own tribe, he thought. Again with the last gasp of his breath, he called out his name. This time there was an answer from the island, and a voice questioning him as to his name. Again Yan called, and then came the sound of splashing water, and in no time it seemed, strong arms were hauling him ashore.

In no time Yan was on a pony and heading for the settlement.

There he found Incres and Wolf holding a council of war, but at Yan's arrival they instantly went about working out how to get Shana back to the island.

"Is she near there?" Wolf asked the boy, as the raft drew closer to the mainland in the midnight darkness.

Yan furrowed his brows. It had been simpler in the light of day, but here in the darkness of night he was not so sure where the girl's hiding place was. "I think over there," he whispered, pointing an unsure finger.

Wolf knew that Incres had not been too keen on them taking the raft to rescue the girl. However, he had seen no alternative if they were to save the flowers that the youngsters had striven so hard to find.

"Yes, in the reeds over there. I am sure it is," Wolf heard the boy gasp.

Cautiously the raft headed for the shore, all the while the rowers' eyes weresearching the darkness for any sign that Hunters might be lying in wait. The sky lightened briefly, and there was Shana, wading out to meet them.

Eager hands, the foremost of which were Yan's, pulled her on board.

"I knew you would come back for me, Yan," Shana cried in delight hugging the boy. Grinning, Wolf gave Incres a sly wink and turned back to his watch.

They turned the raft around and headed for the main beach at the settlement, and were almost there when out of the gloom the enemy raft appeared. An arrow fell short, though a second caught one of the rowers, and for a moment their raft lost direction. Stepping over the dead man, Incres pulled the oar back, shouting at Wolf, who loosed an arrow into the midst of the approaching craft. Wolf gave his friend a grin, as if to say he did not need any instruction on what to do. After all, was he not the greatest of archers? His next arrow was followed by a cry, as the enemy raft drew ever closer.

Incres knew they were out-numbered, and should the enemy get much closer they would soon be in range of their spears.

"There is a half a score against our four, Wolf." Incres blew out his cheeks as he took the strain of the oar.

Yan lifted the dead oarsman's spear, ready to throw it when the time came, and drew the girl behind him. He heard a splash and surmised that Wolf had found another victim. The Hunters' raft came on. He caught a glimpse of pale faces in the weak moonlight and let fly with his spear. A spear landed at his feet and he tugged at it with all his strength, as another flew over his shoulder. He heard Shana scream but dared not turn round, and he let fly with the freed spear. "Over the side!" Incres yelled.

"Make for the shore: it's not too far distant. Go! I will hold them here!" Wolf barked out, fitting another arrow to his bow.

It was then that Incres remembered that his friend could not swim. "Hold on to me Wolf they will not see us in the water."

Wolf loosed another arrow. "No!" he shouted.

Shana stumbled to his side. "We need you to help us get the flowers ashore, Wolf; please don't fail us after what Yan and I have gone through to bring them this far," the girl cried out to the warrior, her voice a mixture of despair as well as mockery, at his fear of the water.

"Come!" Incres called to the one remaining oarsman. "Over this side, before they are upon us!" But even as the man rose he was transfixed by a spear. "Now!" Incres cried, and together they dived into the grey water.

"Incres!" Wolf called out, thrashing the water in panic. There was a shout from the Hunters' raft and someone pointed at the half-drowning man. Incres caught Wolf by the curve of his bow, which hung across his shoulder, and dragged him along an instant before spears and arrows splashed into the water from where he had been.

"Keep silent, you great coward, or they'll know where we are," Incres whispered to the frightened man. "Lie on your back and let yourself float. I will hold you."

Shana swam to one side of Wolf, Yan to the other, and silently in this way they helped guide him towards the shore.

"Keep still; they're searching for us, but can't see us. I believe they're a little downstream of us. Let them search further, then we can be on our way." Incres whispered.

"I'm drowning, Incres," Wolf stammered, spitting out water.

"And I will be happy to let you if you make another sound, you great oaf," Incres hissed into his ear. "Now let me hold your head until they have gone."

It took only a few minutes, but to Wolf a lifetime, before Incres gave the order that they could be on their way, and silently they reached the shore, where ready hands helped them out of the water and up on to the beach.

Exhausted, as much from fear as exertion, Wolf collapsed on to the sand.

"You are not well named, Wolf," Incres laughed down at the shaking man. "At least your namesake can tread water."

Wolf's answer fortunately was inaudible, muffled by the chattering all around him.

"You must be careful, Yan," Wolf advised the boy as they approached the shore in the darkness.

Miroco and his band of half a score warriors were already aboard one of the three rafts which were ready to leave from the main landing place. Two of the rafts were to act as decoys while Miroco, with Yan aboard, would head down the lake and land near to the place where he and Shana had first landed, this raft to be brought back by the four Maru oarsmen

"Incres has chosen you rather than those of the Louma to lead Miroco back to the settlement," Wolf had gone on. It was only partly true what he was telling the boy, for in truth, Inces needed all the full grown warriors to ward off further attacks from Arcana, but he could not tell the boy this without hurting his pride. "Besides, you can run and swim better than any of them."

The explanation seemed to satisfy Yan as he strode on. "Why has Incres chosen this man Miroco, Wolf?" he asked, turning his head to look at his hero.

"He believes that this way he is keeping him and Debu apart. He can't afford to have any trouble between them. We must count on every man we have, young Yan." He gave the boy a gentle push on the shoulder as they neared the waterline. "Now be off with you, and remember what I have said. I shall not see you until your return, for our two rafts will head up the lake and round the island to the northern landing place. Hopefully all eyes will be on us instead of you.

As Miroco put out a hand to help the boy aboard, Wolf gripped the man's wrist. "Make sure nothing is left of Arcana's supplies, and when you've done that, hurry back, for we will need your help here. After four days we will wait each night for your return at the same place as where your oarsmen will leave you tonight."

It was the look on Wolf's face that made the man flinch. "You have my word, Wolf, nothing will be left, not even what Arcana can pick between his teeth." His forced laugh left Wolf wondering if he should be going along as well, even for the sake of the boy.

Yan was glad when they reached their destination. He did not care much for Miroco or his company, least of all their ribald remarks at his expense. At last the time came for the attack upon the Arcana settlement.

Miroco rose from the dead grass where they had lain until nightfall and quietly led his band down the hillside. The settlement gate stood open and unguarded, and as they approached they quickened their pace. In no time at all

Miroco and his band were inside and running to the huts where they were sure the Hunters lay asleep. They were not wrong, only an occasional strangled cry filled the air, as the murderers went about their task. Soon it was all over.

"Now we must burn the place!" Yan cried, his excitement turning to horror at the sight of the mutilated bodies lying in many of the doorways.

Miroco threw his head back in laughter. "Burn the place you say! We shall, but not tonight, and not until we fill our bellies with Arcana's meat and wine. Do not tell me, young Yan, that your belly does not crave the same?"

Unsure as what to say to this fearsome man, Yan crossed the courtyard and threw himself down in a corner.

Yan had thought that he had not fallen asleep, but when he opened his eyes the sun had already risen. In one of the houses across the open courtyard a fox emerged, a severed head in its jaws. Rats scurried away as he rose and crossed to where the storehouse stood. Not that he was at all hungry, but he must gather some food for their journey home, for these drunkards would not be in a fit state to do so. Angrily Yan strode to the fire where Miroco lay snoring, a wine sack clutched in his hand as if fearful of having it stolen.

Taking a lighted ember from the fire, Yan set it to the first of the huts, and when this was ablaze set it to another. This done, he gave a none too gentle kick at Miroco's leg. The warrior gave a grunt, licked his lips and rolled over on to his other side. Again the boy tried to waken him, and this time Miroco opened up a bleary eye at the boy.

"It is time for us to be on our way. I have saved some food for our return journey," Yan told the half-awake man.

Ashes from the burning huts fell on the warrior's chest and in an instant he was on his feet, all sign of any drunken stupor gone. "You've set fire to the huts!" he shouted at the boy, wiping away specks of ash from his wolf-skin tunic. Angrily he kicked out at the nearest sleeper. "Up! Up! you drunkards, the settlement is on fire!"

Slowly the drunken men came awake, those first to do so running to the huts not already ablaze, to snatch what valuables they could from them.

"What are you doing, Miroco? We must be on our way. If you mean to save anything it should be meat, not those trinkets," Yan flared angrily at the man, unable to believe what he was witnessing as the warriors ran from one hut to another.

"Meat for the return journey, you say?" Miroco laughed at the boy. "Who is to say we are returning to your miserable island-eh?"

Yan could scarcely believe what he had heard. "But you came to fight with Incres!. You came here to destroy Arcana's supplies!"

"We came here to fill our pouches with what we could find, then we shall return home. Your island is finished, boy. Had we known how few there were to defend it in the first place we would not have stayed. But now that we are here we are free."

Until Arcana finds you, when - and if, we are beaten," the boy answered defiantly.

"Oh, beaten you surely will be, young Yan, and if you have any sense you will come along with us.

"No, Miroco, I will not betray my friends. And as you say, we are so few and Incres needs every warrior that he can find. He needs you, Miroco."

It was as he finished his last word that Yan felt the dagger in his belly and the look of sheer pleasure on Miroco's face as he thrust the weapon upwards. Sobbing at the man's betrayal of his friends, Yan dropped to his knees.

His last thoughts were of Wolf and Shana and that he would never see them again.

Chapter 6

It was their seventh night of waiting. Incres and Wolf stood by the shore at the foot of the island searching the mainland opposite for any sign that Yan or Miroco were there.

"I fear they are gone, Incres," Wolf sighed. "They should have returned by now."

"The fault lies with me, Wolf my friend. I should have sent more men with them." Incres took a step nearer to the water's edge. Steel grey clouds drifted across the darkening sky. "Wolf shook his head. "We could not afford to send more, Incres, should Arcana strike again."

Incres turned to watch the two girls standing a little distance away. It was strange that the tyrant had not attacked these three days past. He turned back to his friend. "They will not return now, Wolf. It is time that we thought of ourselves."

Overhearing the remark, Gista and Shana let out a stifled cry and fell into one another's arms.

Wolf started towards them to offer his sympathy, halting when Incres motioned him to let them be. He had lost his prodigy, this he had known for a long while but could not let himself believe it. The happy boy was no more, and what made it so hard to bear was that he did not know what fate had befallen him. Silently he followed Incres back up the path.

There was no warning of the approaching storm. Shelters were blown away as if they were no more than leaves from a tree. Incres and Woona with Wolf and many more who had also lost their homes, ran heads down against the wind for the safety of the settlement.

Snow blew across the open courtyard clinging to the wood and the skin doors.

"At least it will send Arcana home early!" Debu laughed.

"Only if the storm bides; it may be gone by the morrow."

"I very much doubt it." Incres turned. He would have to find a new home in this crowded place.

By the fourth day the storm had not abated. The pool that they had filled in the event of a siege was frozen over.

Nedin was busy in the store room when Incres found him. "Shall we have enough to keep us going, Nedin, should this be the start of winter?" he asked the man, forcing himself to be pleasant.

Nedin scowled at his leader. "Only if we tighten our belts." He gave a wide sweep of his hand. "Don't expect all of this meat to keep. We will lose quite a lot."

"I will leave that to you, friend Nedin." Incres's eyes searched around the room. "I'm glad we harvested the corn before the storm hit us." As he spoke Nedin busied himself as if the other was not there. With an effort, Incres controlled his temper at this intentional insult, but pretended not to have noticed. He walked to the door. "I can see that you're busy, Nedin. I'm glad that it's you who is in charge of our lives."

This statement caused the surprised man to look up at the receding figure, and to think once again that Incres had got the better of him.

"Incres! Incres!" Woona ran to him as he stood talking to Trebac and Tomolon, in the centre of the compound. "The lake is frozen, Incres. We have to hack at the ice to break it for water!" she spluttered. "What are we to do?"

The three men looked at one another, each realising the seriousness of the agitated woman's statement, and without a word between them ran out of the settlement to the water's edge.

"Is it thick enough to bear a man's weight, think you, Incres my friend?" Trebac asked looking in dismay at the expanse of white surface.

"If it isn't now, it soon will be, if this weather holds. Last night was colder than ever." Tomolon added forlornly. "We must gather as much wood as we can. Have the women and children help as well. We shall need all that we can get."

Incres faced his two companions. "Should this freeze worsen,

Arcana will simply walk across to our island."

"Then we must fortify ourselves as best we can, Incres. We must seek out what beasts still remain on the island," Trebac added.

"Have a watch put on all the landing places and wherever you think Arcana can land. He now has an option that he did not have before the ice came."

It was a worried leader who turned back towards the settlement. They worked and waited; Nature too grew still as if also awaiting Arcana and his army.

A last they came, a great black horde on a white surface, horns blaring, banners flying, knowing that at last they would reach the island.

Incres halted Wolf and his bowmen as they prepared to plough their way through the snow to the water's edge. "Back to the settlement, Wolf, you cannot hope to halt such numbers; and you must not be caught trying to get back here. The snow is too deep," the leader warned his friend. Seeing the sense in this statement, Wolf ordered his warriors back.

Incres gave the disappointed man a long look. "Let your arrows do their work from within the safety of the walls."

Wolf gave his friend a wry smile. "I only wish that I was near enough to see the look on Arcana's face when he sees our fortress."

Incres walked a little closer to the shore. Black dots grew larger as the enemy approached. "Perhaps if the gods are still with you, Incres my friend, they will open up the ice when they are mid-way across and swallow up all that filth that is the Hunters." It was Debu who had spoken.

Incres had not heard him or his warriors approach, and though annoyed that these men were not preparing for the oncoming attack, decided this was not the time to reprimand them. "I think it best we return, Debu, as I do not think the gods will do as you pray, though if they did it would put an end to all of this."

Arcana did well to hide his excitement as he took his first step upon the island. Now, he thought, there is no escape for this insolent

Maru, and by tonight he would see him slowly tortured in front of his women, and all those who had the gall to oppose the Hunters.

With his warriors plunging through the snow as quickly as they could, Arcana led his men inland, only to draw up in complete astonishment at his first sight of the settlement. Open-mouthed, Arcana stood in awe at the sight of the high wooden walls before him. Clearly the Gods favoured this barbarian. And not for the first time Arcana knew fear of something he did not understand.

"Back ! Back! Get out of range of their arrows!" he bellowed, waving to his equally astonished warriors, who had also drawn to an abrupt halt.

Angrily Arcana retraced his steps until a little distance from the shore, where searching around he shouted for Baracas.

"Yes my lord?" the warrior appeared from out of the clamour of waiting warriors. "Baracas, have the men fell the thickest trees for rams, and get others to build scaling ladders. Have this done by night-fall, for tomorrow we will take that..." at a loss for words Arcana pointed at the walls, "what they believe to be their sanctuary."

"What of the men, my lord, do we build shelters here? Or do we return to our camp on the mainland?"

Further angered by the man's stupidity, Arcana bawled. "And what! Let this rabble escape?"

Baracas gave a slight bow, thinking as he did so that: 'if that so-called rabble had wished to escape, they would have done so by now.' However an ingrained fear of this tyrant bade him hold his tongue, while he still had one.

Woona stood by Incres' side on the firing platform, looking out at the wide circle of camp fires.

"Why, Incres, could they not leave us in peace?" The girl let out a long despondent sigh. "Our island home is so beautiful."

Incres drew her to him. "It is sad, Woona. I believe Arcana himself now wishes that he had not heard of Incres island." He gave an embarrassed laugh at the island that bore his name. "However, that proud man cannot halt until we are beaten, even if it should cost him most of his tribe."

"Many will speak of this when we are gone, Incres." Woona snuggled up to her man, laying her head on his chest.

"Perhaps so, but let us hope, woman, when they do it is a thousand sunrises from now .Come, let us sleep for tomorrow we will need all of our strength."

he knee-high snow was the defenders' ally as the Hunters came at them, impeding their speed as those carrying the rams rushed as best they could towards the gate. On every side, Hunters charged at the walls, scaling ladders at the ready; Wolf and his bowmen scything down those nearest to the gate or walls. Soon the first attack had ground to a halt, warriors struggling back through the snow to where they had first started. The huge felled tree left by the gate.Baracas kept well away from Arcana and his wrath as the chieftain flayed at his Hunters with the flat of his sword, urging the frightened, reluctant men to return to the fray. A few at a time, the line of warriors around the settlement started forward, fellow-warriors shielding the ramp and ladder-carriers from the hail of arrows from the ramparts above. This time, tramping over their dead, the ram-bearers reached the gate, and with a dull thud the ram crashed into the wood-work.

Wolf read the danger and shouting to the warriors from one of the other walls had them fire into the Hunters below, but not before a few of the defenders were themselves brought down by leaning too far over the battlements.

After a few steps back to regain momentum the ram-carriers launched themselves once again at the shuddering, splintered gate. Despite the efforts of the defenders, a hole suddenly appeared in the gate, and a cheer rose from the attackers.

"Time for our fall-back plan, Incres!!" Trebac shouted above the din.

"Not yet, my friend; let the women do their work!"

Women, led by Woona, climbed on to the battlement, handing pots of boiling water to the men, who cautiously but swiftly emptied them down upon the Hunters below. With a scream some of the attackers let go of their burden, and held their scalded faces in their hands, as others, blinded, dropped to their knees.

"Incres!" The cry came from a boy below the battlement. "The furthest wall, Incres. Tomolon says we need men there. They are almost over the wall!"

Not waiting to descend the ladder, Incres jumped to the ground, shouting to those men he wished to follow him.

The young leader was only just in time to see the first head appear over the the timber wall. From the ground below Incres saw Tomolon slash out at the head. In a few moments Incres and his few followers had climbed onto the platform and were slashing and thrusting at those who had reached the top of the ladder. Then, as before, the attack came to a withering halt, and wearily Incres and his men sagged down against the wall.

"The snow is slowing them down, Incres, or their numbers would be over the wall by now." It was as Tomolon said these last words that the first flight of burning arrows landed on the battlements and the gound below. Without needing a warning, women ran to douse the flames, as Incres quickly levered himself off the wall and ran to the gate.   Here the flames had already taken hold where the ram had made the hole in the gate, and with the women supplying the water, Incres and those around battled to extinguish the fire.

Arcana scized his chance; sending Baracas to lead the men, they charged at the ruined gate, some falling as Wolf's bowmen took their toll. More afraid of his master than from the arrows above should he appear to retreat,

Baracas urged on the Hunters, the first of those who, amongst the smoke and flames, had leapt into the compound only to have fallen before as many spears. Still the Hunters came on, Arcana sending more men into the breach. Women from above kept pouring boiling water down upon their attackers' heads and helping to contain the fire as they did so.

"Wolf! Bring your bowmen down here, as quickly as you can!" Incres swung round to Trebac. "See to the walls, my friend, though I believe Arcana means to bring all his strength to bear on the gate.

Watch for my signal should I need your help here."

"And if they get over the wall, Incres, what then?"

Incres gave a shrug. "Then it is all over for us, my friend."

"Then I will see they do not," the man said, grim faced.

Arcana's warriors burst through the burning gate, fanning out into the courtyard as Incres spoke. Wolf's men, ranged in two ranks, the front kneeling with a row behind standing, fired into the onrushing warriors. So unexpected and fierce was the hail of arrows that the few who had managed to survive turned and fled back through the still burning gate, none halting until they were back within their own ranks.

"Get back up on to the battlement, Wolf, I must see how Trebac fares at the wall," Incres shouted over his shoulder as he sped across the open yard.

Trebec saw him coming. "They've gone, Incres. We have beaten them back."

Incres ran up the ladder on to the firing platform and, cautiously peering over the wall, saw with some satisfaction the number of Hunter dead.

"They cannot sustain such losses, Incres," Trebac said with conviction.

"Can we?" Incres turned from the wall.

It was the last attack of the day. Arcana watched unsympathetically as Baracas had his wound tended. "You were inside, why did you not press home your attack? We had those accursed Maru beaten.!"

Inwardly seething with anger that his lord's only concern was his victory and not the loss of his tribe, Baracas made a splay of his hands. "Their bowmen were waiting for us, my lord. Had we stayed to fight none of us would have survived."

"Perhaps that would have been for the best!" Arcana stormed. He grew a little quieter as if what he was about to say gave him renewed hope. "I have sent for all the warriors guarding our back against an attack from the Asan. Even if Meruk thought to harm us, I do not believe he will send his warriors over the hills in such weather. Therefore, with these men and those who will shortly arrive from home, we will see an end to this business."

Have I not heard these same words before, Baracas said under his breath.

An occasional plume of smoke funnelled into the grey of the night sky as Nedin spoke to his leader as he stood by the smouldering gate. "I have divided the meat up. There are many dead and dying." The man's voice was as cold as the night frost. He looked at the damaged gateway. "Is it not time to put up the second gate?"

Incres eyed him coldly; clearly the man had not just come to tell him about meat. "I will do so when it's time."

"It's time now!" Nedin's voice was loud enough for thoseclose by to hear. "Do you mean to wait until we're all dead? Or do you believe that the gods favour you, Incres, and all will be well?"

Incres could have struck the man down, as he had his brother, whose defiance had been less than this. Using all his restraint, Incres replied sympathetically, "I see that you've been hurt, Nedin. If you wish someone else to divide the meat I can have that arranged, so that you can rest."

Outwitted once again, Nedin scowled at his leader, and holding his injured arm, replied with all the hatred he could muster. "I will see to the meat more quickly than you will see to the gate most likely."

As he strode away he heard Incres reply: "each to his own task, Nedin my friend."

Having stood a little way behind Incres, Tomolon had heard the discourse, and moved to the leader's side. "Should that man fear that all is lost here, my friend, then I warn you, you must watch your back."

"Then we must make sure that we don't lose, Tomolon," Incres grinned, though deep down he knew the man was right.

Later, they waited until the moon had hidden itself behind a cloud. Then the ten men, led by Incres, silently made their way through the remnants of the gate. Wolf, Debu and Marc, each armed with his bow, crept a little distance from the gate, arrows pointed at the enemy camp, in case any should stir there, while Incres and the rest of the men quietly and quickly carried the ram back into the fortress.

"Now," Incres spoke softly to the nearest figure at the head of the long line of men and women, and taking the pot of water from one, threw its contents on the snow covered ground outside of the shattered gate and watched it quickly freeze, Wolf with the second pot, and so on until the chain came to an end.

"Think you that will be enough, Incres?" Wolf chuckled to his friend.

"I certainly hope so, Wolf. However, we'll soon see come the morning."

Arcana's army came at them next morning, the warriors carrying a second ram protected on either side by the shields of those running beside them. A cry of triumph went up from their ranks as they saw that the smashed gate still stood as it had been the day before, and they increased their effort as they drew near through the snow, now less deep where they had previously trodden, as simultaneously, the rest of the tyrant's army attacked the walls.

"Now!" Incres shouted to Wolf who, rising from behind the battlement, poured a heavy fire down upon those bearing the ramp, some arrows merely bouncing off the line of shields, though others found knees and shoulders.

With howls of triumph, the Hunters were almost at the gate when the first slipped on the frozen water, bringing down his companion who in turn brought down another and another until the entire column was a sea of arms and legs, the ramp immediately forgotten. Instantly Wolf and his archers were firing into the unprotected bodies, none making it back to their own lines. The attack on the walls and gate had once again failed.

Back on the mainland, Arcana huddled over his fire. He did not look up as the messenger spoke.

"We cannot get through the passes, my lord, not with all the supplies that you require. The warriors you sent for have had to return home. I was scarcely able to reach here myself."

As the shivering man ventured closer to the fire, Arcana started up, his action sending the frozen messenger back in fright. "You were scarcely able to reach here yourself," he mimicked, his face contorted with rage, not so much at the terrified man but at Incres and his gods. Was there no end to that man's ingenuity or better still, good fortune? "Begone before I take my sword to your back, and when your cowardly belly is full, tell those whom you have left that I want those supplies here- Here!" he stormed.

The frightened messenger stared at his chief in disbelief, though he had not the courage to plead that it was impossible, and should they venture forth to try, they would surely freeze to death. Instead, bowing low, the shivering man retreated from the tent.

So, the reinforcements he had sent for would not be coming. Perhaps it was for the best as he did not have the food to feed them. He held his hands over the fire. At last, having come to a decision, he sent for Baracas.

The blizzard had risen in intensity since mid-afternoon, and now for a short time in the darkness of night had abated only to rise again with a ferocity equal to that of the previous day. Making his way along the battlement, Incres halted to inform the freezing guard that he would be relieved shortly. The man, his eyelids covered in freezing snow, peered appreciatively at him as Incres shouted above the rising wind. "I'm going to change the guards as often as I can, that way we will not all freeze.!" The man nodded that he understood, and Incres turned to snatch a quick look over the wall. "We would not see anyone until they were at the foot of the wall in this weather."

"No, Incres,but who would wish to come away from their fires in such weather?" The man shouted back.

Incres turned to step down the ladder. "No, but keep a close look out, my friend, for we must not be taken by surprise", he called out, as he started to descend.

Woona welcomed Incres with a wan smile. Wolf, who was somewhat more cheerful, handed his friend a piece of newly roasted meat.

"This will help warm you up. The blizzard rises, I see. The guards must be frozen.

"That's why I've shortened their watch." Incres squatted down by the fire as Gista and Myna made room for him. "None of you look very happy. Does the weather treat you badly?" Incres bit into the meat as he asked the question.

It was Woona who answered her man. "If we don't have enough to see us through the winter, Incres, what then?...I mean…." she hesitated. "I mean what happens after that? Arcana will only sit and wait until we starve."

"You are worried about this?" Incres spat out a piece of fat, and it sizzled in the fire.

"Not only me," Woona looked around her. "but all of us, especially Nedin. I heard him voice such thoughts as he divided out our fare."

"Nedin! Nedin! Always Nedin!" Incres threw the bone of the meat he had been eating into the fire. "I should have given him the same dose as I gave his brother. Indeed he is more trouble than ever his brother was."

Wolf gave a cough. "He was only voicing what everyone is thinking, Incres. What are we to do when we run out of food, even if we survive the winter?"

Incres seemed to deliberate for a moment. "I think I may have a plan, which should it succeed may help to chase away the fears of many. But should it fail, I believe we are doomed and can only await our fate." And those seated there mulled over his words in silence.

It was two nights before Incres began to put his plan into action. The blizzard had risen in intensity so that it was only those brave enough to venture out, who fought their way to the meat house for their daily fare.

"Watch for our return, though it may be morning at best," Incres informed Trebac. "If not successful, we will wait until tomorrow night. And should anything befall me, you and Tomolon must lead here."

The old man gave a cough against the icy wind, half turning to see if any there wished to challenge Incres's command. When none did, he walked, shoulders hunched as did the others against the wind, up the ladders and on to the battlements.

"The ropes are already over the side," Trebac called out as a blast of wind cut through their ranks. "We will watch out for any of Arcana's guards while you climb down, though I do not believe any will venture to stand outside of their shelters on such a night."

With a wave, Incres lowered himself over the side, saying as he did so, "Remember we will be back tonight or tomorrow night, Trebac my friend."

"And may the gods go with you, Incres."

It seemed to take forever before the last of Incres' men were heading for the ring of camp fires, barely visible through a wind that hurled a thousand icy needles at them. He and his men floundered on, and successfully skirted the first of the fires that burned inside the ring of the Hunters' shelters. No one was on guard.

At last they reached the frozen waters of the lake, and in three single lines, each man held on to the belt of the one in front. Somewhere up above they knew the moon was there, but in this storm everything was a swirling wall of grey. Soon they had lost sight of their neighbouring column.

Incres gasped for breath in the wind. It was all he could do to keep his footing. Even if he should have the breath to call out, no one would hear him above the sound of the storm. They kept going with heads bent, glimpsing only briefly the snow and ice at their feet. He should call a halt, see where they were heading, or at least give the men a rest, but this he could not do, they would only freeze. Perhaps his plan was foolhardy; with half his fighting strength here out on the lake.

For a moment, Incres thought that he had seen a glimmer of light away to his right. Then it was gone. His heart pounded as he saw it again, and hoped that they had not walked full circle.

Suddenly the man behind was down, almost dragging him with him. Incres turned and bent to help the man to his feet and as he did so, others behind the fallen man also fell. He staggered down the line helping those he could. One weakly waved him away, seemingly content to let himself die there. Angrily Incres dragged him to his feet, and they started off again. The light he had seen before was gone.

Incres and his column struggled on. A little way further on he made out a dark shape . He made towards it, and was relieved to see that the leading figure was that of Wolf.

His friend saw him coming and plodded in his direction. "I thought I saw a glimmer of light, over there," Wolf shouted in his ear. Incres gave an almost imperceptible nod, and pointed the way he thought they should go; together both columns made in that direction. Where the third was, no one knew.

It took forever before Incres and Wolf made out the dark outline of trees. Now almost totally spent, the tired warriors moved towards them, and once there took what little shelter they could find.

"I have not seen Marc," Wolf said. Icy particles clung to his lips and face as he spoke.

"I don't know where he is, he could have led his men anywhere in this storm," Incres called back, wiping his face clean of snow. He pointed rather vaguely. "We shall go in that direction. Should we come across Arcana's camp we'll wait for Marc. If he doesn't turn up we will attack without him. We cannot wait forever in this storm."

It was as if the gods were with the young leader, for at that moment through a miniscule of a lull, they saw the glimmer of a camp fire.

Wolf gave a grin, and without a word having passed between, them moved cautiously in that direction.

Impatiently and on edge, Incres waited. He was almost completely frozen. He blew what warmth was left in his lungs into his cupped hands. They would wait for Marc no longer. Wolf unslung his bow, his fellow archers following his lead. Incres drew his sword, and spreading out, heads bent against the storm, headed for Arcana's camp.

Just as on the island there were no sentries; all, it would appear, were inside in the warmth. Incres motioned the first column of his warriors to attack the nearest shelter, while he, with the second column, attacked the next, Wolf remaining a little ways back to cover them with his archers. Simultaneously both parties rushed the entrances.

Incres, leading his party, rushed inside. One man struggled to his feet, an astonished look upon his face as the young warrior drove his sword home. His three companions, scarcely awake, died where they sat, while Incres' warriors dispatched four more that were lying snoring in their beds.

Ignoring the heat of the shelter, the attackers turned quickly for the door, to be met outside by the successful attackers of the first shelter.

Wolf and his men came to join them. "If the gods are with you, Incres my friend, Arcana may be resting his head in yonder tent," Wolf shouted in his ear.

Incres looked around him for a sign that Marc had joined him, for he was uncertain as to how many Hunters might be in the large tent close by, where the lights of several fires could be seen through the skin and wattle walls.

"We cannot wait for Marc, Wolf; the gods alone know where he is."

Cautiously the raiders plodded through the snow to the largest of the buildings, no doubt the dwelling of the Hunter chief himself, and Incres's heart thumped at the prospect of coming face to face with his dreaded foe, the cause of so much sorrow to him and so many more.

It was all over in the briefest of time. There were only seven asleep when they rushed in, but Arcana was not among them . A disappointed Incres was not to know that the tyrant had left for home two days since, during a lull in the storm.

"Was he not there?" Wolf saw the answer to his own question by the look on his friend's face.

"Would that he had, Wolf, then perhaps our troubles would have been over by a stroke of my sword." Incres looked at the dead lying by the side of the fire. "We must be away. The night is mostly gone." He turned swiftly for the door, the rest following. "Debu, have two of your warriors return here with meat to roast, while we load what we find as best we can from the storehouse."

Incres saw Wolf's face light up at this unlooked for decision. "We cannot hope to make the settlement without some food or heat in our bellies," he explained. "But we must be quick."

"Well if it isn't the wanderer returned!" Wolf gasped at the frozen figures of Marc and his column, appearing out of the slanting snow. "They are here now that all the work is done," his taunt bringing laughter from those behind him.

Incres motioned to the man. "Get your warriors inside, Marc, you're of little use to us until the life in you returns."

Leaving the frozen men, Incres trudged as quickly as he and his warriors could to the storehouse. Inside, Debu looked round him in astonishment. "There's enough here to see us all through the winter and beyond, Incres.!" he gloated, striding forward. "It's a pity that we have no ponies to carry it. However, there are poles which will have to do.

"We cannot hope to carry it all back, and it is a pity that we can't burn the rest, for if we were to do so, Arcana's men may see it from the island." Wolf gave a deep sigh.

"This I can do," Debu said with conviction, his eyes gleaming at the prospect.

"How will you accomplish such a task, my friend?" There was a glimmer of doubt in Wolf's voice as he asked the question.

"Some damp wood-sacks of corn close to the fire, then after a while - woosh!" Debu threw his hands in the air to demonstrate the effect.

"Then do so, Debu, but make sure it does not catch until we're inside our settlement, or it will be woosh for us!" Incres gave a sardonic laugh, and the others joined in.

Incres formed them into two columns instead of three as before, each column walking side by side. The man in front was to warn of any danger, as was the man at the rear; these also to act as relief as the men grew tired, and so they set off.

They were less than half way across the lake when the storm abated and the sky lightened in preparation of meeting a new day. Incres hunched the pole laden with meat and sacks of corn higher on his shoulder and quickened his pace. To be caught out here in the middle of the lake would be disastrous.

Later, a long while later, the outline of the island became clearer as they approached. They were closer to the main landing place than he had wished, and Incres pointed that they should veer right, closer to the foot of the island.

At long last they trod the snow of the island, and Incres gave them a moment's rest while he cautiously moved towards the outline of the nearest shelter. It would not be long before the Hunters roused themselves. He drew closer. As yet he could see no one moving about. With the growing light, he could make out the outline of the settlement, the ropes still hanging over the wall where they had left them.

"We must go now. Look out for any guards who might suddenly appear" he whispered to them upon his return. "Wolf: it's up to you now."

Softly Wolf crept towards the settlement. Then, putting an arrow to his bow, with a fox tail firmly fixed to it, let fly, the blunt arrow winging over the top of the wall.

"Now." Incres moved forward, halting behind the first of the Hunter's shelter as some of his warriors did likewise at the second and third, while the remainder of his men struggled under their burdens to the foot of the walls.

At a nod, Incres pulled aside the wolf skin door of the shelter and rushed inside. A moment later he was back outside, plunging his sword into the snow to wipe it clean.

Marc ran to him from the second shelter. "It is a pity we can't just go round and do the same to each and every shelter we come across," he grinned.

Incres gave a grunt. "I'll just be thankful to be back inside our own walls, Debu, though I share your feelings."

Those within the walls having seen Wolf's message, were now pulling up the poles. At the foot of the wall, Incres anxiously scanned the circle of shelters, waiting for the time when someone must appear. One of his warriors saw him and ran to speak to him.

"We've emptied another two shelters of Hunters, my friend Incres. We can hoist up our poles from around the further side of the walls."

"It's good what you have done, but tell your warriors we must hurry. Have some save themselves, by climbing up the ropes. We may need them to defend us from above if we're seen."

No sooner had Incres spoken that the first of the enemy's guards saw them. For a moment he stood there outside of his shelter yawning, then as if not quite knowing what he was seeing, ran yelling to warn the others."Leave what stores are left!" Incres cried. "Get yourselves up the ropes. Now!" he bellowed.

Some, reluctant to leave their spoils behind, continued to help hoist the precious poles. to those above as the first arrow plunged into the snow at their feet: a warning that the enemy were almost upon them. While beside them, their backs to the wall, Wolf, and his archers held off those brave or foolish enough to venture closer.

"Wolf! Get yourself up here!" Incres roared down at his friend as he climbed hand over hand up the rope.

Wolf gave no indication that he had heard, though some of his fellow archers, grabbed at the dangling ropes and started to climb.

As if aware that this was a chance to end it all, the Hunters drew closer, those on the battlements sending a flurry of arrows in their direction, to give Wolf and those who were left, time to start their ascent.

Incres heaved a sigh of relief as he neared the top. To his left, Marc had nearly reached the top when the arrow took him. With a yell of anger, Incres hung there, scarcely able to take in what he had just seen, and how close his friend had been to safety.

Woona ran to Incres as he climbed down into the compound. "You're safe!" She swung to where Wolf had his foot on the last rung. "And Wolf also!" she cried. "We did not believe that it could be done!" The woman's sparkling eyes roamed the returning men.

"Marc is dead, Woona.". As the girl's expression turned to one of sorrow, Incres explained: "An arrow took him as he climbed the rope."

"Look! Look!" The cry went up from the battlements

Together Wolf and Incres climbed back up the ladders to the firing platform, Woona and those close behind her eager to know what had caused such excitement.

"Look there!" One of the watchers pointed to above the tree-line. "Smoke! And not from our island!"

"You've done it, Debu!" Wolf called out, searching for the successful fireraiser. Grinning from ear to ear, Debu appeared out of the crowd. "I thought for a time that I had put too much water on the fire," he addressed his friends.

Smiling broadly,Wolf slapped him on the back. "You have done well, my friend. What will Arcana think when he finds that his stores and camp have gone up in flames, and all he has left are those shelters out there?" Wolf swept a hand at the shelters of Arcana's army that surrounded the settlement

"Perhaps he will come a-begging for some meal to feed his army, Incres?" Trebac laughed.

Incres turned for the ladder. Although this had changed everything for them, the death of his friend weighed heavily on his soul. "May the Gods be with you my old friend," he whispered, and left the others to their rejoicing.

Their camp across on the mainland had gone up in smoke and with it all of their stores. Baracas held his head in his hands. No matter how he built up the fire in his shelter the dark crippling fear within him left him cold with the thought of what his lord and master would do to him should this same man return, having been unable to find a way through the passes. Absently Baracas jabbed at an ember with a small stick of wood. Should the weather hold to its present freezing cold it was unlikely that any supplies would get through, less likely still,,now that the Louma settlement had also been burned.

The despondent man pushed at the ember. Had his master indeed made it through the passes to home? If not he must surely return here. And if so what then?

The only supplies they had were what was here on the island, after that they would starve. Baracas tried to imagine what he must do should Arcana have reached home. Wait until the weather improved and hope for further supplies getting through? Or start back home? Whatever he decided he was a doomed man. He had lost his master's army. The Gods must surely be on the side of this man Incres, and he shivered again at the thought.

Ten days later and Baracas still waited. The weather had warmed a little but not enough to cause a thaw. There was scarcely enough food left to see them home, even if they started out the following day. He had sent two horsemen south, but they had returned with the news that the passes were still blocked. Arcana, it appeared, had won through in those few days when the weather had improved.

Baracas stood at the entrance to his shelter, his blazing eyes firmly riveted on the wooden walls of the settlement. How had that man and his warriors twice crossed the frozen lake in one night in such weather? Not only that, but carrying so much meal and meat that he had seen his men haul over the walls. Again he was convinced that this man was truly protected by the gods.

He had thought of saving himself from Arcana's wrath by attacking the settlement. At least if they failed they would face a quicker death than starving. But should he succeed? The man's face took on a different expression at the thought, that by so doing all would be forgotten. The moment passed, and Baracas' thoughts returned to the present. It could not be done.

They had enough meat, and all were happy. Incres threw a cheery wave at Yan's friends. With the optimism of youth they had apparently gotten over never seeing their friend again; this, and the sad fact of having watched their favourite ponies butchered for meat when things were at their lowest.

Tomolon hurried across the square. "Incres! Incres! Arcana has gone! I saw them cross the lake!" he called out, unable to contain his excitement.

"You're absolutely sure of this?" Incres pulled up before the excited man. "Perhaps it's some sort of trick to have us leave the safety of our walls."

Impatient with this forever over-cautious man, Tomolon rattled on. "No, Incres my friend, they are truly gone, they're already on the mainland travelling south."

"You have seen this with your own eyes, Tomolon? Was Arcana at their head ?" Tomolon shook his head. "Why would they seek to trick us by leaving the island? We would hardly chase after them, would we?" Tomolon eyed his leader, awaiting an answer.

Incres gave a shrug. "We can but wait and see. After all, time is on our side. But you can have our scouts trail them for a little way, just to make sure."

Tomolon was right in thinking Arcana's army was headed for home, and with an outburst of joy the pent-up denizens of the settlement rushed to the frozen lakeside.

Woona too was on her way when she spied Incres by the foot of the wall. She trudged through the snow towards him, a question already on her lips as to what he was doing, then as she drew closer had no need to ask.

"It is Marc," she said sadly, as Incres scraped off the snow from the frozen body. Incres did not answer.

Woona looked away, then over his shoulder at a few more warriors lifting the dead from the frozen ground, while further away others were busy retrieving the supplies that had been abandoned at the foot of the wall. The young woman did not know what to say; she felt awkward, wishing she had stayed with Myna, Gista and Yan's friend Shana.

"What will happen when it thaws, Incres? Some of the tribes burn their dead, unlike us, who bury ours?" It was the only question she could think of asking.

"That is a question only a woman would ask." Incres's words were meant to hurt, a way of dealing with his grief at the death of his friend. "We will do what is necessary when the time comes. Now, do you not have anything better to do, woman, than to ask foolish questions?"

Choking back her tears, Woona turned and ran to find her friends.

Baracas sat astride his mount as the long column shuffled through the snow. For three days they had travelled, and it would take another three days before they came to the deep passes where he hoped the snow might not be so deep as to prevent them getting through. How many by that time would be dead? He had destroyed Arcana's army as surely as had that man Incres. If his lord and master wished to destroy that same man, he must wait until they who had survived were fit and well enough again to return to that accursed island.

Baracas looked over the shambling warriors, but did not really see anything as his thoughts flew to what he himself must do. But first his task was to see how many he could save, after all, the disaster was of his making.

Three days later what was left of the tyrant's army were through the pass and heading for home, but the last they saw of their leader was while he was leading his mount up into the mountains, for Baracas was not likely to face the wrath of his Lord Arcana, no, not ever.

The winter was over: it was time to plant the corn. Disconsolate, Incres swept his eyes over the barren, trodden ground that had been their cornfield. It would not yield as it had done the years before, though they must try if they were to survive. His eyes lifted to gaze beyond the field to the trees cut down for firewood and shelter by Arcana's army. The entire island was almost bare.

For a moment his thoughts were on how desolate a place it had become and should it not be time to move on, but the moment passed. The gods would stir the island to life, and would bring back the animals for them to hunt.

Besides, he was too weary to search for another place to build a settlement like this, and hope Arcana would not find them. No, they would bide.

It was as he was thinking these dark thoughts that he heard an excited commotion from the direction of the beach. For a moment he stood there waiting, then, coming up the path, almost totally hidden by the excited crowd around

him, Incres made out the unmistakable figure of Jude. His heart leaping, Incres strode quickly to meet him and as he did so was aware of others behind the man, one of whom upon seeing him, walked closer to the Maru chief.

"Lyra!" Incres cried, breaking into a sprint.

Jude held up a hand in greeting and without taking his eyes off the woman, Incres returned the greeting.

"Lyra!" He would have taken her in his arms there and then, but the woman had not responded to his welcome, instead of which she acknowledged him with a slight nod of her head.

"Incres." The mention of his name forced him to turn to the speaker. "You are well?" and before Incres could answer, Jude had swung to gaze in admiration at the stout walls of the settlement. "You have done well, friend Incres; this I must acknowledge."

Incres felt his mouth go dry. He had no wish to discuss the matter at this precise moment, for all he wanted to do was to take this beautiful woman in his arms. He could scarcely believe that he was not dreaming. She was here! Lyra was here!

"Do you not think that we should offer our friends some meat and wine?" A grinning Wolf edged through those around to ask his friend the question.

"Yes....yes, "Incres stammered, and for the first time Lyra met his eyes. "Let us go inside."

Incres, Wolf, Tomolon, Trebac and Debu, all now sat gazing at the floor, having heard the reason for Jude and the others being there.

Lord Meruk, Lyra's father, had ordered the boundaries of his kingship to be guarded against the Hunters, who may have had intentions of hunting or invasion.

So that was why, Incres thought, Arcana had not been able to commit his entire force against them here on the island.

Emgot, the first warrior, had been against this, arguing that the presence of Asan warriors so close to Arcana's rear could be seen as provocation. Furthermore, in his opinion, no Asan relished a war with the Hunters, even though this Incres had slain so many that it may have diminished Arcana's power. On the contrary, he had argued, that the Asan should form a pact with Arcana, and to show their sincerity should offer Lyra to Arcana as a means of sealing the pact.

Lord Meruk had vehemently opposed this suggestion, considering it abhorrent that his only daughter should be sacrificed to such a tyrant as Arcana. The argument had stormed on, with Emgot declaring that they, the Asan, should in fact join with the Hunters in destroying all the tribe of Maru, for was it not a fact that they had slain Meruk's only son? And this not withstanding Meruk had let them settle in their land and taught them the art of war, and how to plant the seeds to feed them.

Lyra had told the gathering how next morning her father had ridden off to alert Jude and his Maru by the caves, of the danger they might be in, should some of his tribe supported by Emgot choose to eke out a revenge. Knowing the resentment the first warrior had against them ever since they had first settled there, Jude had realised that hat this could be so.

Here the girl could go on no longer and Jude had taken up the tale of how Lord Meruk had been found slain not so very far distant from the Maru camp. This had been enough for those who until then had sided with their former lord. Now he was dead, apparently by the very hands of those he had chosen to protect.

Only a few, a very few, refused to believe that it was the act of the Maru, but now that Emgot was head of the tribe they dare not voice such an opinion.

Jude had struck camp there and then, and for the next few days the Maru had hidden in the hills on their way here to the island. It was only by the merest chance that they had come across Lyra who, aided by one of her maid-servants, had managed to evade Emgot's clutches.

For a time all was silent as each stared at the earth floor as if seeking an answer there as what to do next. Suddenly Incres rose.

Now he understood the reason for Lyra's coolness towards him; she was grieving for her father.

"We will find shelter for you all. The huts of Arcana's army here on the island are mostly untouched. We only take from them what we need for firewood," he said, stepping to the door. "That is if you mean to bide." Incres let his eyes rest on Jude, his look letting his former leader know that here he was chief of the Maru, or in fact, what remained of them.

"I have food for you, Incres, when will you eat?" Woona asked, as he guided Lyra to the largest of the shelters. Woona gave the woman a smile of greeting. "There is plenty for three." She gestured to her shelter.

"I will see you in the morning, woman," Incres called out to her curtly, as they hurried on. Woona stood as if struck. The meaning of Incres' words had been only too clear. Slowly she began to realise that Incres and this woman were already known to each other. How could she have been so stupid as not to have known? Now it was abundantly clear why Incres had always appeared reluctant to take her to the Asan settlement when they had dwelled by the caves. Tearfully, Woona turned away.

Incres could scarcely contain his desire as he lowered Lyra to the floor.

"My love, here at last! I am truly favoured by the gods." He spluttered, almost choking in his excitement.

Lyra drew him to her, kissing him passionately; Incres's hands shook as he fumbled to undress her, as if afraid that she would suddenly disappear, that it had all been a dream, and that he would not see that beautiful body again.

"Gently, Incres, we have time, you and I" she whispered in his ear. He drew back savouring her nakedness, still not daring to believe that this beautiful creature here was his once again. As Incres began their coupling, he knew that it was not a dream. Or if it was, he must savour it while it lasted.

Though he was loath to leave her, Incres rose and dressed, for there was so much to be done Lyra opened an eye and sat up, the furs around her dropping away from her. The warrior felt his desire rise as he took in her beautiful body.

"You are leaving, Incres?" she purred the words.

"There is much to do. When you are ready you must go to the settlement and break your fast. You will be made welcome there."

"Will I, Incres? I saw the look that woman gave you. Others may think the same." Lyra sat up and rummaged in the bag that she carried with her. In her impatience some of the contents spilled on to the floor.

Incres almost leaped forward. "How come you by this?" he asked angrily, swooping up the carved image from the floor.

Lyra pulled up the fur covers around her, alarmed by Incres' sudden hostility. "It was given me by a tribesman who sought shelter when he and his tribe were on their way home," she stammered, puzzled by the man's interest in such an insignificant item.

"On his way home?"

Lyra made a gesture. "It was some time past when my father was still alive." The woman halted, saddened by the thought. "He said.."

"What was he called?" Incres cut in harshly. "Can you remember, woman?"

Lyra shrank back, suddenly frightened by a side of her lover she had never before seen.Icres relented at her fear. He knelt by the bed. "I'm sorry, Lyra, but it is important that you tell me," he said softly, anxious to make amends.

Lyra looked past him as she recollected "I believe he named himself Min...mir..oh ! I do not know." She clenched her small fists.

"Could it have been Miroco?" Incres asked eagerly.

"Perhaps. He told my father that he and his tribe had travelled from the north to fight with the famous Incres against the Hunters, but this they had been unable to do, as they could not get through Arcana's army to the island, so instead were making their way back home. My father gave them food and shelter, and as a way of showing their gratitude this Miroco gave me this carving. But why does it mean so much to you Incres? Is it valuable?"

"In a way, Lyra. Do you remember the boy Yan, who lived with us at the caves? We saved him, Tomolon and his tribe of Brascan from the storm when they were starving."

"I only vaguely remember." Lyra drew her brows together.

"No matter." Incres went on to tell the woman of how he had sent Yan to guide Miroco and his men to burn the settlement of the Louma where Arcana had stored his supplies. And when they had not returned he had believed that they had failed and had been slain by Arcana's Hunters. Also, he told the woman how Wolf had given Yan the carving as a talisman. Now he was certain that Miroco had slain the boy.

"Then you must give Wolf back the carving," Lyra said softly. "It will mean much that he knows what happened to his young friend."

Incres rose. "This I will do, Lyra. Now I must go."

It was as he made his way around the Hunters' shelters that he came across Wolf.

"Wolf! Wolf" he cried, "see what I have here."

Wolf's glare disturbed him. He had never before seen his friend so stern. "See, Wolf it is the carving that you gave to Yan, Lyra gave it to me. She told me it was given to her by Miroco who spun her a tale that as he could not cross over to our island to fight with us, he and his tribe were returning home."   Incres thrust the small shape at his friend, astonished that his friend scarcely glanced at the object.

"Lyra! Lyra! Would that I had never heard the name!" Wolf spat out the words. What about Woona? Have you no thought for her? She, whom you have shamed in front of all here on the island?"

Incres reeled before the verbal onslaught. "But Wolf, it is Lyra that I love," he pleaded, hoping that his friend would understand.

"No, Incres my friend, you do not love Lyra, you merely desire her. Now with Woona there is a woman who has cared for you, tended your every need ever since I can remember. That my friend indeed is love."

Incres stared at the ground, for he knew that what his friend had said was truly so.

"What can I do Wolf, for I do not wish to hurt Woona."

The mirthless laugh that Wolf gave made Incres look up. "If you do not wish to hurt

Woona then you know what you must do. This, however, I doubt you cannot do; you desire this Lyra too much. Everyone saw how you rushed to your coupling, throwing Woona aside as you would an unwanted rag. I am surely sorry for you, Incres my friend, leader of the Maru." And with this Wolf brushed past his friend.

It had to be done and now was the time, when she was hurting most. Incres walked to the shelter that he and Woona had shared. The skins of the entrance were thrown aside and Woona herself appeared, her face wet with tears, and Incres guessed that by her pale and drawn face that she had not slept.

"I have wronged you, Woona, this I know, and there are no words that I can say to undo your hurt."

Biting back her sobs, Woona's eyes blazed at Incres. "This is the woman you saw when you visited Lord Meruk's settlement? This is why you would not let me journey there with you? This I now understand. You have loved this Lyra all this time. Was it her you thought of when we were at our coupling? Was it her body that you saw rather than mine?" Woona held up a hand, when Incres made to answer, for she did not want to know, even if this man whom she loved were to lie to save her hurt.

"Warriors in our tribe of the Maru have coupled with more than one woman, Woona," Incres said his head bent, staring at the ground, unable to look this wronged woman in the eye.

"To preserve our tribe, Incres. There need be no love between those who do this. Was that all it was between us, Incres?"

Incres' head jerked up. "No, no, Woona , that it never was." He shouted the words, bunching his fists in frustration.

"Then take her, Incres. Have her do for you what I have done since we first knew each other as children of the Maru." Turning on her heel, Woona dipped under the skin covering of the door.

Woona's last words had deeply hurt Incres; that she should remind him of what she had done for him, and that they were both of the same tribe. That Lyra would never be capable of doing what Woona had done for him: he cared little, as

long as he had this lovely creature for himself. Now he must face the others, who also loved Woona in their own way.

Nedin shouted in the compound for all to hear that the Asan had allied themselves with the Hunters and would surely attack them; and now was the time to leave before it was too late.

At any other time Wolf would have laughed at the man, saying, 'here he goes again,' but his thoughts were still on what Incres had done to Woona. He saw Incres walk through the open gate and would normally have gone to meet him, but not today. The man could face this troublemaker by himself.

In no mood on that particular day to listen to Nedin's ranting, Incres pushed roughly through the assembly to face him.

"Nedin, I no longer have the patience to listen to your moaning. Go, and the sooner the better, and take with you those who would follow. But have them know that all your moaning and groaning will not end there," Incres halted to draw breath, " for I swear that should you remain here and I hear another word of dissent from your lips, I will do to you what I did to your brother, whose disobedience to me was as nothing compared with the constant stream of insults that you serve up" Incres' words had grown angrier as he spoke and he took a step forward, his hand on the hilt of his sword.

Nedin's face grew pale as he turned to confront Jude who had been standing nearby.

"You would have him slay me, Jude?" he cried out to the man. "Are you not leader of the Maru?"

"Incres rules here, friend Nedin, and he is your leader since you chose to follow him," Jude answered him brusquely. "Therefore, if you no longer choose to follow him, then it is time that you should leave."

Despite the sadness of the day, Incres felt his heart lift by Jude's acknowledgement of him as leader of the Maru, at least those of the Maru who had followed him as Nedin had done here to the island.

"Then I shall leave. I have no wish to remain here and be butchered by the Hunters and the Asan, one of whom is already in our midst." Nedin turned as he spoke, and at this last outburst Incres could bear it no longer that this man should involve Lyra. Drawing his sword Incres spun the man round. "Perhaps you will die here on the island after all, friend Nedin."

"Perhaps we all will !" someone shouted from the gathering. As one, heads turned to seek out the speaker, who savagely pushed his way through the crowd. "Had you meant to leave, Nedin, you should have done so; now I fear it is too late, for you or anyone." The speaker turned to point in the direction of the lake. " Arcana has come. I myself saw him mounted on his white horse and looking at the island as he has done before."

The news transformed the gathering. Instantly Incres rapped out orders for guards to be put on watch as Wolf made for his friend's side, their ill feelings momentarily forgotten by this new threat.

Later, on the battlements, Incres explained to Jude how the island was to be defended.

"This is a sturdy place you have built, Incres. Will it see off the Hunters as well as the Asan, think you?" the man asked staring out at the activity beyond the walls.

"They will have to land as they tried many times before, Jude.and as yet , until Arcana advises your former friends the Asan, that tribe are not yet aware of our little surprises."

Though it was meant to reassure his former leader, Incres had said it with some misgivings, for although he had almost destroyed the might of the great Arcana and his Hunters, he was less sure of their success now that the Asan were also their enemies.

If Jude was offended by the reference to his former friends the Asan, he did not show it.

"The Maru who came with me will stand by you, Incres, though they are but a half score in number."

"That is all I can expect, Jude. There will be no more warriors coming to fight by the side of the great Incres, I think." Incres gave a wry smirk at his own expense.

"What will happen should Arcana take the island, Incres?" Lyra's eyes were wide with fear as she searched the warrior's face for an answer. "I did not think that he would come again since most of his army were believed to have died in the snow on their way home."

"How came you by this news, Lyra?" Incres asked as he sat on the floor of their shelter sharpening his sword.

"A warrior who had fought alongside Arcana during the storm times, told us of this. He said that he was one of the few fortunate enough not to have frozen in the passes. And how he was on his way home having tired of Arcana and his wars."

Lyra watched Incres as he drew a rag along his weapon. "I remember his name was Baracas, and that he rode a horse, which though lean from the lack of food was very fine." A little of the colour had slowly drifted back into the woman's cheeks.

Incres set down his weapon and crawled to where she sat. "No harm will come to my Lyra," he said kissing her ear as he spoke. "Arcana will never take our island." Thus saying, he drew her to him.

An air of despondency had descended over the island. Now that Arcana had returned, and with the Asan as their allies, there was no chance of their beating back every attack. And even should they successfully defend their settlement, all that tyrant and his allies had to do was sit and wait until they starved.

It was a warm and windless night as Woona skirted the cornfield, corn which the young woman knew she or many of them would never see ripen. Few were about when she entered the settlement walls, and those who were, acknowledged her with

a sympathetic wave. She made for the storehouse where she hoped to find Nedin, and as she drew near saw him at work inside. Whatever failings the man had, inefficiency was not one of them. He looked up as Woona entered the dimly lit room.

"I would have a word with you Nedin, if you can spare the time." Woona stiffened as she waited apprehensively for his answer.

Nedin set down what he had been carrying and leaned back on to the sacks of corn.

"So?" he said with a slight smirk.

Now that the time had come, Woona did not know how to begin. "Arcana…." she began, then halted.

"Arcana?" Nedin teased, sensing her discomfiture.

"We cannot hope to defeat Arcana. This we all know Nedin, and you above all others."

Aware of the flattery, Nedin raised an eyebrow, uncertain where it might lead.

"You have heard that Lord Meruk's daughter has been promised to Arcana as part of the alliance with the Asan. Now that she is here we could…."

Nedin gave a short mocking laugh. "Now that she is here, we could deliver her to the tyrant. Is this what you are about to say, Woona? This of course would have nothing to do with your beloved Incres discarding you for this

Lyra whom you would think nothing of betraying? And if by doing so, you would once more find yourself in the arms of the great Incres,…eh?"

Woona trembled as the man spoke, realising that he had seen through her ploy. However, she must try to convince him that it would be to everyone's advantage. After all, this woman was of the Asan.

"Arcana would be pleased if we could do so, if you yourself could find a way, Nedin . Bargain with him into letting us all here live in peace. Tell him that the whole north and south would hear of how he could have easily slain all here if he had so wished, but instead chose to humiliate the warrior Incres."

Nedin's mirthless laughter filled the large room. "And should I tell the great man this, to his face, do you think he would listen and not have me thrown to the dogs..or worse? Woman, all Arcana need do is wait and he can have this Lyra. But above all he would have your precious Incres in his clutches. This I would dearly wish to live long enough to see," he snarled.

Woona gave a gasp. Oh, how he must hate Incres so much. "Then you will not do as I ask, even at the expense of saving all our lives, including that of your child?"

Nedin drew a deep breath. Perhaps there was a way. "I will think deeply on it, woman, and when I have decided, I will let you know."

Woona's hands would not stop shaking as she sat in her shelter. That Nedin had eventually agreed to her plan had surprised her. He had arranged to have Incres meet with him in the storehouse, but instead he and others would be carrying Lyra to the raft on the shore. Nedin had also suggested that she keep well out of the way, so that when Incres found out that his precious Lyra had been taken, she would not be suspected. Her hand trembling, Woona grasped the cup of wine, drank deeply, and waited.

The deerskin door of Incres's shelter flew open, and Nedin with three men at his back rushed in. In an instant Incres was on his feet, reaching for his sword, only to have it kicked away as his hand was about to clutch the hilt. He took a blow on the back of his head, and as he sagged to the floor heard Lyra scream. His last thoughts before all went black were that Nedin had found a way to slay him.

At first Incres was not aware of where he was until gradually his vision cleared and he made out the outline of a raft, his feet trailing in the soft sand as he was dragged him to the shore. Believing him still to be unconscious they had not bothered to bind him. This, they no doubt would do when aboard the raft.

A little way ahead he saw who he realised was Lyra, her hands bound behind her, a rag over her mouth. They reached the shore, and Incres realised what was about to happen. As one of the men who held him let go of him to steady the raft, Incres swung on his remaining captor, who, losing his balance, fell into the lake. Now his one and only thought was on how to rescue Lyra. In a flash he was on the man who held her, throwing him aside and pulling her away.

"Run, Lyra run! Back to the settlement! Save yourself!"

"What about you, Incres?" the woman screamed at him.

"I'll deal with them. Now run! For your very life!" Incres swung to confront his captors, Nedin to the fore, a spear thrust out before him. "You will not slay me Nedin, even if in your heart you would wish to. But it would not sit well with your plan, would it, Nedin, my friend? Arcana would not thank you. Perhaps it will be your head on a spike instead of mine, traitor to the Maru!"

Nedin drew back, his hand shaking with anger as he held the spear. The man was right: he could not slay him, even though every fibre of his being wanted to.

As Incres lunged at Nedin, he knew nothing of the man who had crept up behind him, only the blow on his head from the club, then blackness as he fell.

Woona wept uncontrollably, Nedin had betrayed her. Wolf put an arm around her to comfort her, but she drew away. She had slain the only man she had ever loved. Now Arcana had him. She shuddered at the thought of what Incres might be suffering at this very moment. Incres would be long in dying. Wolf too, looked more sad than she had ever seen him. No jests, no laughing comments. She felt sick. It was all her doing. And all the time the woman Lyra was safe, saved by Incres, so she had said.

"I will take a walk, Wolf." Woona rose from where she had been sitting in her shelter.

"Shall I come with you?" Wolf asked softly, his heart broken for both his friends.

Woona shook her head.

Wolf nodded his understanding, his misery compounded as he recalled his last meeting with his friend; the harsh words spoken to him of how he had treated this woman who loved him dearly and could not bear the thought of losing him.

Outside Woona walked slowly through the line of trees, where already there were signs of new life. All could have been so different had Arcana left them in peace. And now that he had the man who had humiliated him before the eyes of all, would he leave them be, or would his vengeance not be satisfied until they were all dead or in slavery? Sobbing, Woona thought of Gista, Myna and the young girl whom Yan had loved. What would befall them? She shuddered, her sobbing sending night birds into the air. She had done this thing. She would never see Incres again.

The sobbing woman was at the cliff edge before she realised how deep had been her thoughts, and how far must she have travelled from her shelter. Below, the silent lake lay, a shimmering grey-blue mirror. She lifted her head to where the lights of Arcana's camp glowed across the water, as if they too were mocking her for her folly.With a last look across the lake, Woona let herself fall down to the water below.

Epilogue

Jude heard the rustle amongst the bushes. He moved cautiously forward, his spear at the ready. Wolf was too far away to come to his aid with his bow. Slowly the branches parted and the shape of a ragged man appeared, his face almost hidden by an unkept beard. Horrified by such an appearance and not a little apprehensive, Jude took a hasty step back.

"Jude, you cannot be afraid of me," the voice croaked.

Startled by the stranger speaking his name, Jude peered at the face through the bushes, though he thought that he had recognised the voice.

"It cannot be you, Incres?" Jude took a hesitant step forward. "We saw your head on a spike across the water those years back when Arcana took you prisoner." For this surely could not be the man whom the gods had forsaken.

"The head was that of Nedin who had betrayed me. Arcana spared no one. Not even his child."

Jude clutched his spear tighter as the stranger continued. "Arcana did not attack the island, there was no longer a purpose to it when Lyra died." He halted at Jude's gasp. "I was told she died by throwing herself into the lake. Then, as Arcana did not attack the island, Emgot took his warriors home; he would not attempt to take our island by himself"

While Incres spoke, Jude now began to understand why Arcana had left them alone. The tyrant had believed it to have been Incres' woman Lyra who had died and not Woona.

"And you Incres, what happened to you? Why did Arcana spare you?"

"Spare me? You call this sparing me?" Incres thrust himself through the shrubs holding out his arms, arms without hands. As Jude reeled back in horror, Incres came closer. "He took me to his land in the south and had me caged like an animal, so that all should see with their own eyes the man who had defied him, and of the Lord Arcana's vengeance."

"Then how come you to be here, friend Incres? How did you escape...especially..."

"Without aid of my hands?" Incres finished the sentence for him. "It is a long story, but not all who live on Arcana's land love him, Jude. There was such a man who was not of the Hunters and who had tried to escape with his wife. They had been caught and Arcana had her slain. The man himself had been crippled as a warning to others. It was he who planned my escape. It was his way of seeking revenge on the great man." Incres paused for breath. "And now I am home again, back to my island."

This Incres should not do, Jude decided. Arcana would surely know that Incres would return here, to this his only home, where others would care for him. And should he also discover that Lyra was not dead he would surely return. This he could not let happen, not let it start all over again.

Jude felt a deep sorrow for the man and all that had befallen him since his taking. And in that briefest moment Incres also knew what he was thinking. Incres stood there as if past caring what would happen to him. And as these thoughts seeped through his mind, Jude's spear took him in the chest and he sank to the ground.

Quickly Jude hauled his former tribesman back behind the bushes and had only just done so when Wolf returned from his hunting.

"You have caught something, friend Jude?" Wolf pointed to the bloody spear. "Almost, Wolf my friend, but it won free."

Wolf gave a chuckle. You are growing old, my friend Jude. It is time you passed your knowledge to someone younger."

"Such as yourself, Wolf? If so, may the gods have mercy on the Maru." Jude forced himself to laugh.

Wolf put a hand on Jude's shoulder, and began to lead him away. "No, not myself, but there is one who in a few years time may take that place. And if he takes after his father, he will indeed lead the Maru wisely.... although"

Wolf laughed loudly, "I am glad that he does not bear his father's looks but those of Lyra his mother! Now let us return to Incres Island before the sun sets."

Lost in their own inner thoughts, the two men set off on their journey home.

The End

Copyright. W.G Graham 2013

Printed in Great Britain
by Amazon

37697511R00108